Blind Love 001

A Romance Novel by

BENNA ELSE

BLIND LOVE 001:
A Romance Novel by
Copyright © 2024 **Benna Else**

ISBN (Paperback): 978-1-958475-45-4
ISBN (Ebook): 978-1-958475-46-1

All rights reserved. No part of this book may be used or reproduced by any means, graphic, electronic, or mechanical, including photocopying, recording, taping or by information storage and retrieval system without the written permission of the author except in the case of brief quotations embodied in critical articles and reviews.

Because of the dynamic nature of the Internet, any web addresses or links contained in this book may have changed since publication and may no longer be valid. The views expressed in the work are solely those of the author and do not necessarily reflect the views of the publisher, and the publisher hereby disclaims any responsibility for them.

Printed in the United States of America.

PROMINENT
BOOKS

5830 E 2nd St, Ste 7000 #9983
Casper, WY 82609
USA

CONTENTS

Chapter 1
Old Pals | 1

Chapter 2
The First Meeting | 4

Chapter 3
The Preliminaries | 11

Chapter 4
The Beginning | 21

Chapter 5
Wedding/Married Life | 54

Chapter 6
The Second Honeymoon | 79

Chapter 7

Where's Jami? | 92

Chapter 8

Where is Nikki? | 106

Chapter 9

Good News/Bad News | 116

Postscript | 127

CHAPTER 1

Old Pals

"Jami, you're crazy." Dave looked at his friend's face. He could see that he was sincere but he couldn't believe Jami's last statement.

"I'm serious. If men would stop thinking with their reproductive parts and think of women as intelligent human beings, maybe the divorce rates wouldn't be so high. Relationships would be healthier and stronger. I sincerely believe that marriages would be happier and last longer."

Dave leaned back in his chair, smiling at his friend's statement as he muffled a chuckle.

The two friends were having lunch and for some reason, they'd gotten onto the subject of relationships. Dave had known Jami since high school when they both played on their high school basketball team. After graduation, they attended the same university where Jami was premed and Dave was focusing on business management.

"I know you're laughing at me," Jami told him. "But I've met your wife Leigh, and you can't tell me that your first thought when you saw her was 'How do I get her into bed?'". Jami smiled broadly.

"You know, I guess you're right," Dave said, after reflecting on his initial encounter with Leigh. "Yes, I just liked the way she spoke. Her British accent fascinated me. I enjoyed our conversations."

"My point exactly. You became friends first, right?"

Dave nodded. "Again, I have to agree with you. So, is that why you've remained single all this time?"

"Yes, I think so. I'm searching for that special someone who will be friends with me first then we can move on from there. Also, she'd have to be willing to deal with my disability. Not many women want to be married to a blind man."

Here they were now both thirty-four years old and still the best of friends. The major difference was Dave was happily married to an Asian woman he'd met in England, and Jami was a criminal attorney having had to switch his major when he began losing his vision.

"Okay, I get your point. I've told you that I have this friend who I think would be perfect for you."

"Yes, you've told me," Jami said. "But she's got to be gorgeous having been a model, and now you tell me that she's a successful real estate broker. She could have any man she wants. Why would she be interested in someone like me?"

"Hey, man don't sell yourself short. You're a good-looking guy, intelligent, and you've got a great personality."

"That could fit almost any man with vision—and other men could tell her how lovely she looks or how beautiful her outfit is. These are things I wouldn't be able to do. Not really."

"Jami, I wish you'd stop using your disability as a handicap. You manage your life very well. You're a partner in a successful law firm, have a beautiful home, and financial security."

"Speaking of work, I've got an appointment to get to—don't you have a staff meeting at your office?"

Dave glanced at his watch. "Yikes, where did the time go?"

"I'll pay for lunch Dave, and I'll see you and Leigh at the benefit on Saturday night, right?"

"Yes, we'll be there. Thanks for lunch—I owe you." Dave grabbed his coat as he stood. "We'll talk tomorrow, okay?"

"Call in the evening," Jamie said. "I've got a heavy caseload all day tomorrow—and you don't owe me anything."

"Thanks, Jami. I've got to run." Dave hurried from the restaurant

Jami stood up and placed cash on the table to cover their lunch and tip. After slipping into his coat, he extended his cane, and he began making his way out of the restaurant. The hostess bid him a good day, and he returned a smile and a nod, before stepping out on the sidewalk.

Jami inhaled deeply. It was a cold February day in Chicago and he felt like walking. Turning to the right, Jami proceeded toward his office. He needed to prepare his closing argument for tomorrow and visit one of his clients who was now serving time.

CHAPTER 2

The First Meeting

Nikki carefully applied her eyeliner as she leaned toward the make-up mirror. She wanted every detail to look perfect. After all, she was modeling a beautiful outfit for her friend, Connie.

Nikki smiled at her reflection before applying the lipstick. Her painstaking application of makeup had achieved success. It had been many years since she'd taken so much time to be this glamorous. Her daily routine was tinted moisturizer, mascara with eyeliner, and lip gloss.

But tonight, because of the benefit and the silent auction, she wanted to do justice to her good friend's gown. If Connie's creation sold, many of the guests would be interested in her other designs. She was already making a name for herself and this additional exposure would help.

Minority Professionals of the Midwest sponsored this event each year. The money from the silent auction held during this benefit would provide financial aid and scholarships for exceptional students who graduate from high school but can't afford to pay tuition and high fees for college.

The attendees were people from not only the financial sector but also fashion-forward movers and shakers. Several philanthropists, millionaires, retail store owners as well as the elite in the legal and medical fields supported this annual event.

BLIND LOVE 001

Also, Nikki thought, *I'll get to see my dear friend Dave.* It had been over a year since they'd seen each other. He'd gone overseas for his company where he'd met and married his wife, Leigh. Even though she'd been invited, Nikki had been unable to attend because her mother had to have emergency surgery. Tonight, she would finally get to meet Leigh for the first time and get a brotherly hug from Dave. Nikki looked forward to a great evening.

Nikki entered the ballroom of the Sheraton Hotel wearing a long, warm, black wrap. After checking in with the officials, she strolled around the grand room, noting the variety of items available for the auction. Articles were displayed on long, white cloth-covered tables at one end of the room.

The variety of items amazed even her. From time-shares to a new car, clothing, and technical equipment were all to be bought for the right price. Each item was assigned a number and a minimum suggested price.

Once the auction officially opened, Nikki checked her wrap, received her assigned number and began making her way around the crowded room. Nikki held her number in her right hand at about waist high. The gown she was modeling was number seventy-six.

As more people arrived, the atmosphere of the room seemed charged as if an electrical current pulsated just below the tiered crystal chandeliers hanging from the fresco ceiling. The maze of guests smiled as they whispered into jeweled ears and cologne faces. Since this was a semi-formal occasion, the men wore dark suits or tuxedos, and the women colorful gowns or dressy pant-suits.

It had been years since Nikki had received so much attention from strangers. When she began her modeling career, she attracted a great deal of attention but that had been at least ten years ago. Now she just enjoys selling commercial and residential properties. Having a successful career without some of the temptations that came with the fashion industry was a relief.

As she passed among the guests, she answered questions regarding her dress. *This will make Connie so happy,* Nikki thought. Connie was a gifted fashion designer but very shy. They both hoped that with this showing, someone in the fashion industry would help escalate Connie's dreams to much higher success.

"Hey, number seventy-six," a male voice called out, and Nikki knew immediately who it was.

"Dave!" she said as she turned to greet her friend. He looked as handsome as ever with his close-cropped hair, dark brown complexion, and puppy dog eyes. He hugged her gently.

"I don't want to mess up that dress," he said as he stepped back looking her up and down.

"Dave! I'm so happy to see you at last. You look great!"

"I have to agree with you. I do look great. But so do you," he said with a warm, inviting smile. "It was challenging finding you in this crowd. I asked the woman at the desk where I could find the most beautiful model. She directed me to another model. So, I had to return to the desk to ask again. They directed me to you." His smile widened. He always liked to tease Nikki.

"Thanks for keeping me humble. Well, how are you? How are things going? Where is your lovely bride?"

"Whoa, hold on, everything is great. Leigh is with a group of friends that I want you to meet. Maybe you can broker a real estate deal," he said as he took her by the hand.

Nikki knew he was kidding and being with him reminded her of old times. They'd met years ago while taking a photography class at the community college. They had been partners during a couple of class projects. Their friendship grew, and when the class ended, they stayed in touch. They would occasionally go out to dinner or a movie. After she began dating Ron, they lost contact.

Her breakup with Ron was painful, and she didn't want to see or talk to anyone. It was over a year before she happened to run into Dave. They rekindled their friendship, but it was always platonic.

"So how does this silent bidding thing work?" Dave asked as they made their way through the crowd.

"It's easy. Each item has an assigned number so all you do is get a bid card. Write the number of the item on the card that you're bidding on, add your information, and the amount of your bid. Give it to those people sitting at the tables at the front of the stage. They record the bid for each item, and the highest bid for a particular item gets it."

"That sounds easy," he said.

"It is. What I think is great is that you don't know if you've got what you want until the end of the benefit. Someone could outbid you."

"I knew there had to be a catch. It sounded way too easy."

BLIND LOVE 001

"Have you found something you like?" Nikki asked. She noticed that Dave was leading them to a small group of well-dressed people.

"Yeah, more than I wanted to find."

As they approached the group, Nikki couldn't help but notice a tall, handsome man speaking rather seriously to those around him. His tuxedo and white on white formal shirt emphasized his physique. *That's either an expensive rental or he's paid a fortune for it*, Nikki thought.

When Dave and Nikki joined them, all of the men looked at Nikki with approval. All, that is except the gentleman who had been speaking. He only afforded her a fraction of a glance before turning away then continued speaking without glancing her way again,

The stranger's curtness piqued Nikki slightly and yet, she found it somewhat refreshing. Because of her good looks most men were enticed immediately with her. That usually meant their conversation would be superficial, shallow, and biased, only leading to some sexist remark.

Nikki didn't mind a look of approval, but what she hated was ogling which had been one of the main reasons she'd gotten out of modeling. She'd wanted to do something with her life other than to look beautiful and be fussed over.

She was intelligent, a hard worker, and enjoyed working with the public. She often volunteered at soup kitchens throughout the year, not just during the holidays, always ready to assist where needed.

This guy didn't seem to notice her, and that made him different in her eyes. *I'll apologize to him when I'm introduced*, Nikki thought. His demeanor made her want to meet him. He had acted the complete opposite of most men.

When there was a break in the conversation, Dave began by introducing his wife to Nikki. Leigh was gorgeous with long, straight, dark-brown hair, and almond-shaped eyes. Her olive complexion was flawless. Dave had told Nikki once when they'd talked over the phone that his wife's mother was of Philippine ancestry and her father was from Barbados.

Dave continued with the introductions until he finally got to the man Nikki had immediately noticed.

"And finally, this is my best friend, Jamison Bledsoe."

"I'm happy to meet all of you," Nikki said. "I apologize if we interrupted you, Mr. Bledsoe."

"No apology is necessary," he said and nodded in her direction. A woman asked him a question, and he immediately turned his attention toward her.

Nikki didn't know quite how to react. Was she being self-centered because one man was treating her as an average-looking woman? She had to admit, she was. Except for Dave, most men couldn't take their eyes off of her. But his guy was different. As she listened, she discovered that he had a wonderful voice, and she also found him even more handsome than she originally thought. The fact that he wore tinted glasses made her curious.

Nikki knew that she needed to be walking about but she just couldn't seem to pull herself away from this group. Then a lovely young woman joined them and gently touched Jamison's arm. He leaned in her direction as she quietly told him there were some people he needed to meet.

"Lead me away," he said with a smile after excusing himself from the group.

Nikki watched as they retreated arm in arm. As Jamison and the young woman made their way through the crowd, he lowered his head toward his companion as they shared words. He laughed, rich and deep, making Nikki slightly envious. That was the first time in her life she felt any amount of envy toward anyone, especially another woman.

As the group began to disperse, Nikki, Dave, and Leigh made plans to get together the next day. Leigh wanted to place a bid, so after hugs, they walked away while Nikki resumed her modeling. She didn't get far before another male voice, not quite as pleasant as Jami's, penetrated Nikki's thoughts.

Nikki reluctantly turned around with her best smile. It was Merl Swinson, a short, small-boned man with a great deal of clout. He owned an exclusive women's store on the Avenue. He is also associated with many influential people in the fashion world. Nikki politely gave him the information he requested though her thoughts were still on Jamison Bledsoe. There was something about Jamison that she'd found appealing.

"Nikki," Merl said, while his gaze roamed freely over her body. "Connie's creations are getting better, but you…you truly do this gown justice."

Nikki was unimpressed by his comment. He'd said nothing she hadn't heard before. But she didn't want to alienate him, so she offered him one of her more dazzling smiles, which he readily accepted.

A couple of years ago, Merl had purchased some of Connie's formal designs. However, Nikki knew that Connie tended to be irregular in her production, and she'd lost many possible clients.

"Nikki, I want to market Connie's designs in my stores exclusively. Do you think I'll have the same difficulty with her?" he asked.

"Not anymore, Mr. Swinson. Connie has matured and is more consistent in her work ethics. Yes, she sabotaged her own success but all that has changed. She also has more help."

As they continued their conversation, Nikki caught sight of Jamison. He was talking to some women, while the young lady who'd walked away with him was still at his side.

"Mr. Swinson, do you know that tall gentleman standing over there?" Nikki asked.

Merl followed her gaze.

"Oh, yes, that's Jamison Bledsoe. He's a renowned criminal attorney. Haven't you heard of him?"

"I just met him tonight. Do you happen to know that young woman in that burgundy dress standing next to him?"

"I think that's Jonell Bledsoe," Merl said as he peered over the eyeglasses that perched on his strawberry-shaped nose.

Nikki's heart sank. He was married. But isn't that the way it goes, she thought. All of the good-looking ones are always taken. Then Nikki quickly chided herself for this line of thinking. She hadn't considered marriage at all, not since Ron—and that was almost nine years ago. Although the pain was slight it was still with her. She forced herself to focus on Merl.

"Nikki, turn around again, please," Merl requested.

She complied as he studied the gown. *Is he really looking at this dress or how I look in it?* Nikki wondered as she pivoted.

"And you're absolutely sure Connie will be able to keep up with the production demand for her creations? I intend to market this item extensively—and I'd want to see her other designs."

"I can definitely assure you that Connie is more reliable," Nikki said.

"That's reassuring. I need her to make ten of these dresses. What other colors does she have this dress in?"

"Is there any reason why you can't call her? I'm just here to model this beautiful gown. You can ask her all of your questions. I'll tell her that you'll call her on Monday. Would that be alright?"

Nikki just wanted to move on. She was tired of talking to Merl, and she needed time to think. Why hadn't Dave mentioned that his best friend was married?

After bidding Merl goodbye, Nikki continued her stroll about the room. She saw Jamison throughout the evening with his wife by his side. She also got glimpses of Dave and Leigh, and she saw how happy they were together. *Am I truly happy with my life?* Nikki asked herself.

By the end of the evening, Nikki was aware that the highest bid for the dress was $3000. Connie would be pleased. With a successful evening behind her, Nikki took a taxi home. Exhausted from walking in high heels, she slipped into a warm bath to soak the tension away.

As she relaxed Nikki reviewed the evening. Several men had attempted to talk to her about things unrelated to the gown. The one man whom she wished had found her attractive never afforded her more than a glance. Except for Ron, her first love, Jamison had awakened feelings that she thought were gone forever.

Ron had been married but that hadn't stopped him from taking her virginity. She was young and inexperienced in the ways of the world. Nikki had begun modeling at the age of sixteen. She met Ron when she was nineteen and had never really dated.

Ron was mature, and he romanced her with expensive gifts, compliments, and dates at exclusive lodges. Nikki didn't listen to her parents, she listened to her heart. Ron had inherited a great sum of money and was the head of the company that his father had founded. He was the man of her youthful fantasies—tall, dark, and Latin. Unfortunately, six months after their trip to Brazil, she learned that he was married, and he and his wife had an understanding of mutual infidelity as part of their marriage arrangement. Nikki terminated their affair.

Humiliated, she moved away from home and refused to go out socially while berating herself for being such a fool. Deep despair and depression followed as the months passed. After that experience, Nikki determined never to give her heart to anyone again.

CHAPTER 3

The Preliminaries

For Nikki, Sunday was always a day to relax and especially after a long night on her feet. Picking up her cell phone she checked her voicemail and was happy that there were no urgent messages. Next, she phoned Connie.

"Hullo," a soft, sleepy voice said after the fourth ring.

"Wake up, sleepyhead," Nikki spoke quietly into the phone. "I've got great news for you if you want it."

"Nikki! Oh, God, how did we do?" Connie said, now sounding fully awake.

"Not me, but you—and you did great!" Nikki said gleefully. She could hear items falling. Nikki knew that Connie often fell asleep with her sketch pad on the bed.

"How great?"

"Well, the highest bid for the dress was $3,000! Isn't that fantastic?"

"Three thousand? You're kidding me, aren't you?"

"I'm not kidding, but that's not the best part."

"There's more? Tell me, tell me," Connie pleaded in a sweet high-pitched voice.

"I don't know if I should. I'll bet you went to bed early while I was up walking in fashionable shoes to show off that sexy creation of yours. I think I deserve some thanks," Nikki teased Connie.

"Thanks. Now in God's name tell me more," Connie begged.

"Your favorite businessman was in attendance. He loved the gown and wants you to have more in his office in two weeks."

"Two weeks! Is he crazy? I'll be dead trying to do that in just a couple of weeks. Who does Merl Swinson think I am?"

"Maybe superwoman? I suggested that he give you a call. So, expect to hear from him soon."

"Nikki, hold on, I've got to go to the bathroom. You woke me out of a sound sleep."

Nikki could hear Connie's footsteps shuffle across the floor. Connie lived in a loft apartment which was perfect for her. There was one large room that was divided by a chest-high brick wall. The majority of the floor space was filled with dressers, mannequins, a drawing table, two long cutting tables, three sewing machines, and a serger used for fancy stitching.

While waiting on Connie's return, Nikki's thoughts drifted back to last night, to Jamison Bledsoe—the sound of his voice, his laugh, and his carriage. *Drop dead gorgeous*, she thought.

"Hi, I'm back," Connie said. "Now I can focus. Isn't it amazing how when you have to go to the john really bad, you can't think?"

They both laughed, then Connie asked, "Now tell me, do you know who bought the dress?"

"Yes, Mrs. Collins. She and her husband own Collins Industries. Very North Shore, so you need to come get the dress and have it cleaned asap. She wants to have it by the end of the week. They're traveling for a month."

"Is she your size? Will I have to do alterations?" Connie asked.

"I don't know. But I've got her contact information. I'll text it to you. I think she was a little wider in the hips."

"I'll come and pick up the dress later this morning. Are you going to be home?"

"Until 1:30. I'm meeting Dave and his bride at their apartment this afternoon."

"Really, how's Dave doing—and is his wife as lovely as I've heard?"

"Yes, to both questions."

After ending their conversation Nikki got up to dress for her daily run. She knew that would help her have the energy to get her through the rest of the day. But all during her run, she couldn't shake the thought of the man from last night. *When I get to Dave and Leigh's, I'm going to ask him why he didn't tell me that his best friend was married,* Nikki thought. As she continued jogging, she kept thinking of ways to bring up the subject.

That afternoon Nikki walked toward the apartment building where Dave lived. It was sunny although the wind made it feel very cool. She wore slacks, a turtleneck sweater, and a leather jacket. Her shoes were very comfortable compared to what she'd worn the previous night. As she approached the high-rise building, she saw Dave talking and laughing with a tall man. Nikki couldn't believe it. Jamison Bledsoe was leaning against the rear door of a black Mercedes Benz. He and Dave seemed to be having a funny conversation because both of them were doubled over with laughter.

There was a third man dressed in a black jacket over a white sweater, and black trousers, but he was standing at the front of the car. This man was extremely tall and muscular with a smooth, dark brown complexion. The closer Nikki got, the larger and more menacing he appeared.

However, Nikki wasn't concerned with him, she just wanted another chance to speak to Jamison. So, quickening her pace, she approached the men.

"Hey, Dave," she called as she got closer to the two friends.

"Nikki! Is it time for you to be here already?"

"I think so. Leigh did say 1:30, didn't she?"

"That's right. Yikes! Jami, how long have we been talking?" Dave asked.

"Say, man, I'm not your timekeeper—and that's what you get for being away for so long," Jami teased warmly.

"Which reminds me," Dave said as he walked toward the other man. "I've got to ask Hannibal something,"

"Hello, Mr. Bledsoe," Nikki said, smiling as she extended her hand. She liked the taupe trousers and dark green, knit sweater he was wearing.

His response was polite but impersonal. He didn't acknowledge her extended hand.

He turned away from her and called to Dave, "I've got to go. Tell Leigh that I enjoyed having lunch with you both. Hannibal let's get moving." Then he opened the back door of the car, but before getting in he said to Nikki, "Ms. Townsend it was nice seeing you again." Then he smiled.

Nikki felt her heart quiver. That smile was a killer.

Dave joined her by the curb, and they both watched the black sedan move away.

"Well, let's go upstairs. I'll bet Leigh is upset with me. I was just going to say goodbye to Jami half an hour ago. He'd treated us to brunch today," Dave said as he gently touched her arm heading them toward his apartment building.

Nikki wasn't really listening to Dave. Her mind once again was focused on Jami. There was something about him, but she couldn't quite put her finger on it.

"Hey, honey, guess who I found?" Dave said as they entered his apartment.

"I'll bet it was Nikki, but you're still in trouble," Leigh scolded in a loving tone. "You said you'd be up in five minutes. You were supposed to help me set up the dessert tray."

"I know, and I'm sorry, but you know how it is with me and Jami. Best friends for years, and it's just good to be with him again. So, what can I do to help now that I'm here?"

"Hello, Nikki," Leigh said with a warm smile. "Please make yourself at home. Our place isn't very large, but hopefully, we'll find something bigger soon. And you, my dear husband, please finish getting the coffee tray ready while I show Nikki our little abode."

Dave saluted his wife playfully before planting a kiss on her lips. Leigh took Nikki into the living room which was small but cozy.

"We just have one bedroom, but it's fairly large, and a nice sized bathroom. But Nikki, you're in real estate, would you help us?"

"I'd be happy to do that. Just tell me what exactly you're wanting. Do you want to buy or rent—and what area of the city do you want to live in? Chicago has a lot to offer."

"Thanks, we're still trying to figure that out. I want to work, so I'm starting to look for employment. I think once I'm working then we can see what we can afford."

"That makes sense and besides, you really haven't seen much of Chicago, have you?"

"That's true. We've only been here for a couple of months. Moving my things from England was very stressful."

Dave entered the room with a large tray of goodies. Placing them on the coffee table, he then sat down in a nearby chair. Both Leigh and Nikki sat on the couch.

Three mugs of coffee, different packets of sweeteners, and tiny pastries adorned the tray.

"My goodness, this looks so good. You didn't really have to," Nikki said.

"It's no problem," Leigh said, "I enjoy having company, and except for Jami, we really haven't had many visitors."

After taking a sip of coffee, Nikki asked how the two of them met.

"I'll tell her that if you don't mind, honey." With a nod from Leigh, Dave began, "I'd been in England a few weeks working like crazy. Some of my co-workers asked me to join them. They were going to a party and they thought I needed a break, which I did. Anyway, there must have been a hundred people squeezed into this tiny apartment.

"Dave, there weren't a hundred people. You're such a mess," Leigh said with a smile.

"OK, maybe not a hundred but a lot of people. Anyway, I was just checking people out when I saw her. She was talking to some women. I just approached her and asked if she could excuse herself from her friends because I needed a favor."

Nikki glanced at Dave with a questioning look. Then she shifted her gaze to Leigh who was smiling at her husband. "A favor?"

"Yes," he answered, then looked at his wife. "*I'm a foreigner in a strange land and need to be rescued by a lovely lady. Will you rescue me?*"

"And she fell for that?" Nikki said laughing. "You've got to be kidding me."

"Well, no, not really, but she laughed. That was enough."

"Yes, he was so sweet and sincere," Leigh said. "We talked the rest of that evening. He asked me for my phone number and email. We dated for some time, and he proposed. And well, here we are."

"That's a wonderful story. I wish I could have attended your wedding, but my mother had to have emergency surgery. I'm sorry I didn't make it."

"If you don't mind, we could show you our wedding pictures. We've got them on video."

As Nikki watched the wedding pictures, she saw the love and joy Leigh's family showed toward Dave and his family. It wasn't a large gathering, maybe about 50-60 guests, plus family. The wedding cake had yellow and lavender-colored icing. The groom's cake was white icing with dark blue flowers.

Then there was Jami giving the toast to the newlyweds. Just as handsome with his tinted glasses, dark gray suit, pale gray shirt, and blue and gray tie. Nikki stared at his image. She'd had only one lover, and he'd broken her heart. As the years passed, she never allowed herself to have feelings for another man. But this Jamison Bledsoe was a different kind of man.

"Wow, that looks like I missed out on a fun event. And I saw someone who was very pregnant."

"Yes, that's my sister." Leigh smiled as she related, "She had that baby two days later. I was happy I didn't miss the birth. My sister was in labor during the wedding, but she had promised me that she wouldn't miss it. It was amazing she didn't have it that same day."

"And I saw your buddy, Jami," Nikki said.

"Yep, and that brings me to something I want to ask you," Dave said as he placed his coffee mug on the table.

"This sounds serious," Nikki said.

"It isn't serious, but you've met Jami. What do you think about him?"

"What do you mean? I've only seen him very briefly. So, I really…." She couldn't quite put her thoughts into words.

"Look, I'm trying not to be a matchmaker, but I've always thought you two would be a great couple. I've told Leigh, and even she thinks you'd be a good match for Jami."

"But Leigh, you've just met me. How can you think Jami would be a good match?"

"I saw how you looked at him last night. And I caught you looking at him at different times throughout the evening. You were so funny and sweet."

Nikki felt embarrassed because she didn't realize anyone was watching her.

"But isn't he married? I mean the woman that was with him most of the night. Isn't she his wife or girlfriend?"

"Oh, God no! That's his sister Jonell Bledsoe."

Nikki couldn't believe what she was hearing. Jami was single!

BLIND LOVE 001

Trying to maintain her composure, she folded her hands in her lap, her mind reeling. She had been fantasizing about that man all last night and this morning. Now here is his best friend asking if she would consider dating him.

"But Nikki, before you answer you have to know that Jami has a disability."

"What do you mean? He looks perfectly healthy to me," Nikki said.

"Well, he's gradually losing his vision. He has retinitis pigmentosa. It's a condition that causes a person's retinas to gradually degenerate. Usually, the progression is quite slow, but in his case, for some reason, it has been pretty fast, lately. He has peripheral vision but is considered legally blind."

Nikki couldn't speak. All she could do was look at Dave and Leigh in disbelief.

"I know this is so much to take in, but I care about him. He gets depressed sometimes. Before this all began, he and I were on the basketball team in high school, and we went to the same university. It was so gradual at first, but then he began missing some easy basketball shots. He finally decided to go to an eye doctor. To say the least, he was angry. He was majoring in medicine, planning on being a surgeon like his father.

"To make things worse, his then-fiancé broke their engagement because she didn't want to be married to someone with a disability. He dropped out of school not really knowing what to do or where to turn. I don't remember ever seeing my friend so upset. He tried to continue driving until he was in an accident. The idea of being dependent on others angered him all the more.

"It was amazing he didn't get killed. His parents were devastated but his father had the presence of mind to come up with a plan. Dr. and Mrs. Bledsoe sent both of us on a trip around the world. His father reasoned that before Jami lost his vision, he should see some of the beauty of this planet. My parents helped some with my expenses but Jami's parents are wealthy.

"Nikki, I'm telling you this because I know you've sworn off being with someone in a romantic way but even if you'd just be his friend, I think it would be good for both of you."

No one said anything for a while. Nikki was trying to absorb all of this information. Yes, she'd found Jami very appealing. Listening to him speaking he sounded very intelligent. But blind, that put a different spin on her thoughts.

"Is there a surgery that can correct this vision issue?" Nikki asked.

"None that I know of."

Silence.

"How bad is his eyesight?"

"Things in front of him he can't see, but peripherally he's good," Dave said.

Nikki turned to Leigh. "Leigh, you've been with Jami. What was it like when you first met him?"

"To be honest, he is gracious and very careful with his movements when out in public. He knows that he has limitations but for the most part, most people don't realize it. Of course, he has a dog named Max. But as Jami says, the dog is just for show. He's funny and I just really fell in love with him. He's a very nice guy."

"So," Nikki asked Dave, "who was that man with you two when I met you guys downstairs?"

"Oh, that's Hannibal Jackson," Dave answered. "He's Jami's houseman, cook, chauffeur, and, at times. his bodyguard."

"What do you mean bodyguard?"

"Jami is a criminal attorney, and some of his clients are raw."

"Let me get this straight. Jami Bledsoe is legally blind, a criminal attorney, not married, and he doesn't have a girlfriend. And you think I'd be a good match for him?"

"Yep."

"Why me?"

"Because you're intelligent, easy on the eyes, you have your own money, and you wouldn't take advantage of him. He's dated over the years, but most of the women wanted him for his money. Plus, you two look good together." Dave smiled.

Nikki didn't know what to say. Yes, she was attracted to Jami, but would she really want to be with someone who had a disability? She was an active woman, who liked to jog, swim, and attend exercise classes. She also liked to dance, go to movies, and read books. What did she know about helping a person who was legally blind?

"I know what you're thinking, Nikki. I'm not asking you to marry him, just get to know him. I think he needs to have a good woman in his life. He usually just hangs out with his law partners, Hannibal, and, now that I'm back, with me."

"I don't know, Dave. I mean, he seems like a nice enough guy, but I don't think I'm the right person," Nikki said.

Leigh chimed in, "Nikki, please give Jami a chance. I understand why you're reluctant. But I think you'll be surprised."

"Listen," Dave said, "My folks are having a get-together next weekend. Why don't you come? I know Mom and Dad will be happy to see you. It's been a long time and it will be fun. Jami will be there, and you can get to know him. What do you say—please?"

"All these years I've known you, why haven't you mentioned Jami and his disability before?"

"Well, I guess when we met, you were pretty down on men. And to be honest, I'd hoped we'd be more than just friends. As time passed, it never seemed to be the right time. First, it was you not wanting to have anything to do with men. Then, Jami complained about how women were just gold diggers or money hungry. And some, to be honest, just wanted sex because he's a good-looking man. But now it seems the time is right. I'd hoped you two would meet at my wedding but that didn't happen. So, here we are. Come on, what have you got to lose?"

Nikki looked at her friend and his wife in wonderment. Their anticipation was apparent. She was surprised and flattered that they both seemed to care about her and Jami.

"I still don't know. I need to think about this. I've never even been around anyone with a disability."

"We understand," Leigh said. "But please come next week. I really haven't met many people since I've been here. We could get to know each other better. What do you say to that?"

"I'll check my calendar. I think I'll be free next Saturday, but please don't get your hopes up. This scares me a little. Dave, I'd love to see your family again, it has been a long time. And yes, Leigh, I'd like to be there for you. We do need to get to know each other better, especially since Dave and I have known each other so long." Nikki smiled. "Thank you both for this afternoon. To say the least, it was informative and loving. I've got a lot to think about."

Nikki changed the subject to get the attention off of herself and onto Dave and Leigh. She asked more about England and Leigh's family. Then she asked Dave how his family enjoyed having a daughter-in-law from another country and of a different ancestry? After staying for more than two hours, Nikki finally said goodbye.

Walking home, Nikki questioned the idea of a possible relationship with a legally blind man. He had to be over six-foot-two, broad-shouldered with a tight waist. It was apparent that he worked out. His manner of speaking and his sincere laugh, Nikki found alluring. Well, if as Dave suggested, they could just be friends, that wouldn't be so bad. Except for Dave, she'd never had a male friendship. Would that even be possible? After the heartbreak with Ron, she had vowed not to let her heart dictate her relationships with men.

For the past few years, her focus has been to be successful. She'd chosen real estate because it was something she knew where she could achieve success, and she had. Just as she had been on top in her modeling career, now she was at the top of the real estate world in Chicago. She sold and managed commercial as well as residential properties. It kept her busy and out of the arms of the men who pursued her. She had a good life so why mess it up?

CHAPTER 4

The Beginning

The following Saturday was cold with high winds typical for the first of March in Chicago. Nikki waited in the lobby of her building for Dave and Leigh to pick her up. She had also gotten her friend Connie to come. She thought it would be a good idea to have a backup friend with her.

All this week as busy as she was, Nikki hadn't stopped wondering how this possible friendship with Jami would begin. How did he feel about having her as a companion? Would he be opposed to the idea? Dave or Leigh never said if they had suggested anything about her to Jami.

Finally, she saw the SUV Cadillac pull up in front of her doorway. All the windows were tinted so she couldn't see who was inside. Opening the back passenger side door, Nikki's mouth dropped open. There sat Connie and next to her, behind the driver's seat, was Jami. Also in the back cargo area was a beautiful dog.

"Well, hop in," Dave said from the front seat.

"Wow, you've got a carload," Nikki said, hoping no one noticed her surprised expression when she opened the door.

"Hannibal got involved in a project, so Jami ended up coming with us," Leigh said from the front passenger seat.

"Of course. Hi, Connie," Nikki said, hugging her friend. "And Jami it's good to see you again."

"Thanks," Jami said. "I've been looking forward to this family reunion. And I guess Connie is going to be the new addition to Dave's growing family."

"Hey, that's right. Connie, you're my new sister if that's alright with you,"

"*I am?*" Connie said. "That's great because I don't have any siblings. It's always been just me and my father. This is going to be fun."

With the radio playing rock & roll, the conversation was boisterous. Jami and Dave were fun as they reminisced about their years in high school, and the tricks they'd played on each other and their teammates. Dave's parents lived in a Chicago suburb called Evanston in a lovely, single-story brick home on a large lot.

As they piled out of the vehicle, Nikki noticed several cars already parked along the curb and in the driveway. She also noticed Jami as he made his way to the back of the Cadillac to get his dog.

"Have you got everything?" Dave asked Jami.

"Yep, I'm good. I know this place like I know my own home," Jami said.

Leigh got a large basket out of the back of the vehicle while Dave got folding chairs. He handed one to Jami saying he couldn't use Max as a reason for not carrying anything. Nikki and Connie were handed blankets to carry. After locking the vehicle, Dave pulled a wheeled cooler.

Nikki walked behind Jami, watching him as he made his way toward the house. She couldn't help but like what she saw. She also watched Max guiding him as they approached the stairs leading to the front door. It was teamwork as Max stopped, letting Jami know there was something in front of them. Jami seemed to understand and began going up the stairs. The front door flew open and a big robust man stood in the doorway—Dave's father, Mr. Johnson.

"Jami! It's good to see you again," he said before giving Jami a welcoming hug. "Say, who are all these people behind you?" he joked.

"I don't know. I guess they like my dog so they just followed me here."

Mr. Johnson greeted everyone. He hugged Nikki, saying she needed to visit more often. When he met Connie, he shook her free hand gently telling her how happy he was to meet her. And, of course, he hugged and kissed Leigh on the cheek telling her how beautiful she looked. He added,

BLIND LOVE 001

"I still can't understand how my son could be so fortunate to have such a lovely wife."

Mr. Johnson's compliments made Leigh blush and Dave beamed.

"Dave, my son, you're a fortunate man. So, what's in the cooler?"

"Beer, of course," Dave replied before getting the bear hug from his father.

There were many people in the big house so it took a while for introductions to be made.

Jami seemed to know most of them because they were Dave's family. Nikki also knew quite a few, so she introduced Connie. Leigh had met some before when she and Dave had Skyped with many of them before their move to the States.

Dave's mom appeared from the kitchen to greet and meet the new arrivals. Nikki kept watching Jami. A number of women came up to him—talking to him, touching his arm or his shoulder. They were flirting with him, and he knew it. Nikki wanted to approach him but decided to wait. They had all day.

The house had an open living and dining room. At the back of the dining room were French doors that opened onto a large glassed-in porch, which stretched across the back of the house.

The television and bar were located in the basement. Quite a few of the men were there watching a game. Jami went down as well.

Nikki waited a few minutes before following him. From the bottom of the stairs, she watched. Dave was sitting next to Jami and when a play occurred, not only did the TV sports commentator call the play, Dave would put his own spin on what had happened. Jami seemed to understand exactly what was going on during the game.

When it came time to eat, Mrs. Johnson had all guests clean and sanitize their hands. It was buffet style with the tables lined up along two walls in the dining room. Jami didn't get any special treatment, he was in line with everyone else. But Nikki stood in front of him to tell him what his choices were.

After getting a full plate, Nikki offered to guide him to a seat.

"Thanks, I've got a place on the porch." He smiled. "Max is holding my spot."

"OK, I'll be Max and get you to your chair. Do you want me to carry your plate?"

"No, I've got it."

Outside, Nikki found Max lying by a chair with a small table next to it.

Jami placed his plate on the table before sitting, and Max moved out of the way to make room for Jami's legs.

"Can I join you?" Nikki asked.

"Do you want to?"

"I wouldn't have asked if I didn't."

Jami smiled. "I like that. You know that we're being set up."

"Yes, I know. But Dave's our friend and he's happy with Leigh. I think he wants two of his best friends to also be happy."

They were sitting across from each other with the small table between them. Nikki watched as Jami carefully checked out the location of his food with his fork. At times, he'd tilt his head.

Nikki inquired, "May I ask how much you can see?"

"Well, I can't see you because you're right in front of me. But if you were next to me, I could see you. It's weird, I know, but it's my life."

"How long has it been like that?"

"It's so gradual that it's hard to say. I do remember being able to see until my junior year of college. I started missing basketball shots that I shouldn't have. Went to the doctor, got diagnosed. And the rest, as people say, *is history*." Then he scooped up his baked beans with his fork and ate.

Nikki followed, enjoying her meal. They talked about their careers and how much they appreciated their jobs.

Nikki said, "I love the journey—finding the right property for my clients, and the closings, seeing the joy on their faces. That's what I enjoy most about real estate."

"For me, it's my *closing* argument. When I know my client is innocent, I will reason with the jury. I've been fortunate to be successful. However, if I have a client who is guilty, I'll still give a good defense, but I try to see if I can get a deal. I try to be an honest attorney. And yes, I know that's an oxymoron," he said with a chuckle.

They both finished their food and Nikki got up to take their plates away.

"You don't have to do that."

"I know, but I want to. Do you want another beer?"

"No, I'll need to take Max for a walk. He's been very patient."

"Could I walk with you?"

"Of course."

Nikki disposed of their plates. Then she searched for Connie who was deeply involved in conversation with two women. They were talking about fashion and cosmetics. Nikki just told Connie that she was going for a walk.

After getting her jacket and Jami's sweater they headed for the front door. By now the sun was getting low in the sky. It wasn't as windy but still quite cold.

Jami knew of a doggie park not far from the Johnson home. They didn't talk as they walked the two blocks to the park. Once inside the double-gated off-leash area, Jami released Max from his harness to let him run free. Nikki found a bench and they sat down.

"Why are you spending this time with me?" Jami asked.

"I find you interesting. I'd like to get to know you better."

"Say that sounds like what a man says when interested in a new acquaintance."

"Wow, I guess it does. I didn't mean it that way. It's just I've never known anyone who is blind. To be honest, I'm also curious what made you decide to go into law."

"Originally, I'd planned on being a surgeon, following in my father's and grandfather's footsteps. Then this thing happened with my eyes, and after getting over the anger and depression that followed, I knew that I still wanted to help people. I looked at my options, and law was what I liked—criminal law really piqued my interest. That's about it. Now it's your turn. Why real estate?"

"I'm not talented like my friend Connie. I like people and helping them get something that will make them happy. I can work as often or as little as I like. The office I'm associated with deals with high-end properties, so my commissions are sometimes amazing. And I'm sure Dave told you, I'd been a runway and print model, so I invested well. Please don't think I'm bragging. My parents helped me with my investing. I took college courses on that subject also."

"So do you just handle commercial properties?"

"No, residential is more fun, especially when it's a first-time buyer. I'll give a basket full of goodies to my clients when they purchase a home. I find it good PR. But to answer your question, I do at times work with commercial investors." Nikki glanced toward Max. "Uh-oh, Max is taking care of business. I'll get the poop bag to clean up." Before Jami could object Nikki was on the move.

"How would you have picked that up if I hadn't been here?" Nikki asked when she returned to the bench.

"I'd keep him on the leash. He's trained to go on command. So, I'll say *get busy* and he does."

"Wow! I don't know what to say to that."

Jami decided they should be getting back. He called Max and put the harness on him after the dog quickly responded. They returned to the house party.

Just before entering, Jami stopped. "Nikki, how would you feel about going out with me?"

Without hesitation, Nikki said, "I'd like that."

"Next Wednesday?"

"What time?"

"Around five o'clock—I like to beat the dinner crowd if that works for you."

"Where will we meet?"

"Text me your address and I'll pick you up."

Wednesday came quickly, and, with Hannibal driving, Jami was prompt. He texted her that he was waiting in the car in front of her building.

Upstairs was the name of the restaurant and that name was appropriate. The lobby was on the ground floor but the restaurant was on the second level. Booths with high backs lined two walls while the center of the room held tables with seating for four or six customers. There was also an alcove with two booths where they were seated.

Jami knew what he wanted to eat. He confessed that he'd pulled the menu up online and used the *text-to-speech* feature. He explained that he didn't read braille and he didn't like to ask whoever he was with to read the entire bill of fare. "But Nikki, you take your time."

Nikki looked at the large selection on the menu. Finally, she opted for chicken Kiev with a side salad. Jami asked for the beef stew with salad and he also ordered a carafe of wine.

Their conversation was easy, and he listened carefully showing genuine interest in what she said. He even asked questions if he needed clarity.

"So, you closed on a large warehouse this afternoon?"

"Yes, that building had been vacant for several years. It was my listing and my sale, so I don't share the commissions except with my broker. But that's okay."

"I'm impressed." Jami smiled.

"I've been doing most of the talking so now it's your turn."

They brought their food before Jami could begin. He tilted his head slightly to see his food before he began eating. As they ate, he talked between bites. Nikki learned that he'd gone to jail to visit a client and then he had gone to court for another case. The day before, he had worked late into the night because his client's parents worked until seven in the evening, and he needed to share some information about their daughter's case. "The father wanted to pay me in cash but I know they don't have much money—so I told them not to worry. He's a proud father and doesn't want to be a charity case. Like he said, 'I'd have gotten a public defender if I'd wanted one.' So, I took what he had but I'll save it. If I win or lose, I'll return the money. They're good folks, and their daughter just got mixed up with some *bad* people."

After their meal, Jami and Nikki went arm in arm for a walk. Without Max, Jami had his cane.

Jami had explained that he likes to walk after an evening meal. Nikki was ready, having worn comfortable boots. They both wore warm coats and Nikki had a knit cap while Jami had on one of wool.

Nikki wondered what Jami thought of her. He said he could see her but he couldn't see her clearly. Then he shared with her that, back when his vision was better, he had seen her.

"When was that?" Nikki asked.

"A couple of years ago. Dave and I were leaving a restaurant and he spotted you walking past. He caught up with you and the two of you talked briefly. I saw how beautiful you were, and I've held that picture of you in my mind ever since."

Nikki stopped dead in her tracks. "So, you've known since the benefit who I was, and you acted as if you didn't."

"Yes, but there was a reason. From Dave's ravings about you, you sounded too good to be true. I needed to be sure. Nikki, I've dated a few women, but I've never clicked with anyone the way I have with you. I know you may not believe me but I'm sincere when I say there's something about you. And I've waited a long time. I'd hoped we'd meet formally at Dave and Leigh's wedding. So please give us a chance to be friends. That's all I ask."

Nikki didn't know if she should be flattered or angry. She'd been enjoying their time together, and she was becoming accustomed to his mannerisms. How he navigated when eating or just walking still amazed her. His attitude toward this visual challenge seemed to be upbeat although she was sure he had times of depression.

But now he was informing her that he'd been aware of her for more than two years. What was he thinking? And that's what she asked him.

"Not very clearly," he confessed. "I've been apprehensive for years about dating. As I said, the few women that I've been with seem to always want something from me. One woman told me that she needed to help her mother with credit card debt. She promised if I could loan her the money, she'd pay me back within a month. We'd been out a few times, so I thought I knew her and could trust her."

"How much did she scam you for?"

"Not so much, just $2000. But it was the idea that she felt she could get money from me. Naturally, when the month was up, she somehow didn't have the money to pay me back. She apologized and flattered my male ego, but the red flags were there. So, I stopped calling her, although she continued trying to contact me for weeks."

After listening to this experience Nikki could, in a way, understand his caution. "But Jami, all women aren't like that. She was just one."

"Oh, I know, but I've had a couple of other experiences that were not healthy. So, I'm a little gun-shy. That's why I just want us to be friends."

"Okay, that's fine. It really is good. It takes the pressure off, doesn't it?"

BLIND LOVE 001

"Yes, that's what I think. We can just enjoy each other's company."

※

Their friendship had begun with caution. After that first date, Jami phoned Nikki the following evening. He shared his day and asked her about hers. Nikki found it easy to talk with him. He shared an experience with an acquaintance who had gone on a radical weight loss program.

"Are you kidding me?" Nikki exclaimed.

Jami laughingly said it was true. "He said that he'd lost so much weight, he could get both of his legs into one of his old pant legs."

"Jami, you're too funny."

"Yes, but I thought it would make you smile."

"Well, you accomplished your goal. I smiled. Thanks."

"So, what are you doing this Saturday? Could we have dinner?"

"I tell you what—how about we do something different?" Nikki asked.

"Like what?"

"It's still pretty cold outside, but how would you feel about going to a museum?"

"But I can't see that well."

"I'll be there to help you understand and the museum has audio so the different exhibits are described in detail."

"Nikki, I don't know. Since my vision has gotten more challenging, I guess I've played it safe. I try not to draw too much attention to myself. I probably sound fearful. But I'm not, it's just stepping out of my comfort zone."

"Jami, I think I understand. I just want you to widen out. Why not give it a try?"

※

One Saturday a month Nikki would meet with her crew. That also included Leigh, now that she'd become Dave's wife, and their friendship was growing. On this particular outing, they did a spa day, then lunch. It was Connie's turn to select the eatery, and she decided on deep-dish pizza.

"You've got to be kidding me!" Phillipa exclaimed. "You know how I always eat too much. Why are you tempting me?"

"Because it's my turn, you can order salad and I've got something to celebrate." Connie seemed to glow.

"Really?" Nikki asked.

Connie nodded with a broad smile. The four women walked toward Rush Street to their favorite pizza restaurant, anticipating excellent food and good news from Connie.

Once seated and drink orders made, three pairs of eyes turned to Connie.

"Okay, okay, I'll tell you. As you know Merl Swinson has been carrying my designs exclusively. About a week ago, he told me that the top buyer from Saks Fifth Avenue talked to him about my gowns. She wanted to know if I also designed a ready-to-wear line." Connie paused to inhale.

"Don't stop now!" Leigh exclaimed.

Connie grinned. "Merl spoke to me. I'd been thinking about the possibility of a casual line of clothes. To make a long story short, I signed a contract with Saks yesterday!"

"What about Merl? Is he upset?" Phillie asked.

"No, because he's also going to carry my ready-to-wear line of clothes. Isn't this the best news ever?"

Words of congratulations and hugs for Connie were abundant. Also, a call for champagne cocktails was ordered. The four friends ate, drank, and talked for over two hours. Phillie, the name her friends called her, spoke of her travel agency which she co-owned with her boyfriend Jonathan. They had some great deals for trips to the islands of the Pacific as well as Mexico.

"That sounds great." Leigh said, "But until I get a job it's not going to happen for Dave and me."

"What type of work are you looking for?" Phillie asked.

"I'd really like to work as an event planner. I especially would like to plan weddings or anniversary celebrations.

"Yuck," Phillie said. "Why? People get married, and, two to five years later, they're getting divorced."

"Wow, Phillie, is that why you and Jonathan have never married?" Nikki asked.

"Yes."

Nikki looked closely at her best friend. Phillie had told her of living through the bitter divorce of her parents. And that she'd never marry and cause so much hatred between two people who'd once professed to have loved one another.

"Maybe I could help you," Connie said.

Leigh frowned. "What do you mean? How?"

"Saks has a bridal department, and I'm sure Merl knows people that may be able to help you," Connie said. After a pause, she asked, "Have you worked as a wedding planner before?"

"Yes, back home I worked a couple of years as an assistant to the owner of an event planner. She specialized in weddings."

"Okay, I'll check around this next week. If you don't hear from me by Friday, call me."

"Oh, Connie, thanks so much," Leigh said.

"By the way, Nikki, how's Jami doing?" Connie asked.

"We're doing good."

"Still just friends?" Connie teased.

"Yes, and we're both comfortable with that," Nikki said. She then shared some of the fun things they were doing. She'd gotten Jami to jog outside, where before he would run on his treadmill in his basement, and they'd even tried tandem bike riding.

"Phillie, I want to get with you and Jonathan soon," Nikki said. "We can have a double date sometime."

"That sounds great."

So, their friendship grew as Nikki introduced Jami to being open to trying different activities. Saturday and Wednesday became their time together. When they went to the movies, Nikki explained anything that Jami didn't quite see or understand from the movie's dialogue. As the weather got warmer, they attended baseball games. Jami listened to the play-by-play over a portable radio with an earpiece. Naturally, their walks were almost endless. They'd even gone clothes shopping together.

They would double date with Dave and Leigh, or with her good friend Phillipa and her live-in boyfriend Jonathan. They were becoming best friends. Jami would invite her over to his house for meals that Hannibal would prepare. It was always delicious, and that made Nikki envious of Hannibal's skills in the kitchen.

As their time together was becoming more familiar, Nikki decided Jami needed to have a new experience.

"Jami, what do you think about parachute jumping—you know, skydiving?" Nikki asked, during their afternoon stroll in Lincoln Park.

"What do you mean, what do I think? I've never even considered it."

"Well, I thought it would be fun. It's something we could experience together for the first time."

Jami stopped walking, turned, and faced Nikki. "Are you crazy?" He asked in his usual calm voice. "Have you ever done it?"

"No, never. But I have a friend who did and she invited me to watch her take her first jump. It looked thrilling! I've thought about it, but I never got around to actually doing it. I've done some research, and I think you and I could do it."

Jami began to chuckle, then he seemed to realize she was serious. "Honey, I'm not sure. I am legally blind, so how could I do it?"

Nikki led him over to a park bench to sit down. "We would jump in tandem. You'd be harnessed to an experienced instructor, and so would I. We can go to the airport, talk to an instructor to see if it is really something we could do. Oh, Jami, I want our friendship to be extraordinary. What do you say?"

"I'll think about it. You got me to ride a bike which I thought I would never do again. And that was fun being on a bicycle built for two. But jumping from a plane, that's an experience I don't know if I'm ready for."

"Will you at least give it some serious consideration?" Nikki pleaded.

***

Now the three of them, Hannibal, Jami, and Nikki were on their way to the small airfield. Jami had thought about the idea of skydiving for several days and Nikki hadn't pressured him. But he knew it was something she wanted them to experience together.

Since they'd been seeing each other, their dates were getting routine. Dinner dates, movies, jogging some mornings, talking for hours over the phone. They both liked the idea of trying new things. That's how she got him riding the bicycle and rock climbing. Now, a parachute jump!

"Jami," Nikki said as she cuddled next to him in the backseat of the car, "you'll enjoy the feeling of free-falling, floating in the air. My friend fell in love with this sport."

"I'm glad for your friend but why haven't you done it?" Jami asked.

"To be honest, I've let my work get in the way. But we've taken the lessons and Terry has been an excellent instructor for you, hasn't he?"

"Yes, he has. It's just that I tend to like my sports activities on the ground." Jami smiled. "I'm teasing. I'm really looking forward to this new venture. After this, I may try for my pilot's license."

Even normally quiet Hannibal laughed out loud at that statement.

The laughter seemed to ease the tension. Nikki and Jami felt their relationship growing stronger. For Jami, who usually had his guard up whenever being introduced to something new, this was major.

Arriving at the airfield, they exited the vehicle and to their surprise, Dave and Leigh were waiting. "What are you doing here?" Nikki asked.

"Well, we couldn't miss this event. I've got my camera and I'm recording every minute," Dave said.

"How did you know?"

"Hannibal called last night. We knew you were planning on jumping but we didn't know when or where," Leigh said. "So, Dave made Hannibal promise to give us the information without your knowing."

"We're glad you're here," Jami said with a smile. "And if anything bad happens, make sure Max and Hannibal have good homes."

After laughing and hugging each other, they walked inside the hangar. A few of the jumpers were already seated. Jami and Nikki joined them while their friends took seats in the back row.

Terry, a slender man about fifty years old, ambled into the hangar greeting everyone with a warm smile. After making his way to the front, he waited patiently until all conversation had stopped.

"Good morning, everyone. We've got a beautiful day for skydiving. For the new people, please go to the back where those chairs are," he said, as he pointed in the general direction. "I'll be there in a couple of minutes to give you additional instructions. Those of you who've jumped before and want to go now, pay Sally in the office. And for you observers, you can get some coffee or just wait, I won't be long."

Terry did a quick review of what they had learned. The safety rules, how to exit the plane, and what not to do—in other words, not to panic. Nikki and Jami held hands as they listened. Terry also had them do a practice jump from a platform down onto a cushioned mat.

Before long, they had their gear on and were heading for the plane. Jami would be in tandem with Terry while Nikki would be with another instructor. It took several minutes for the Twin Otter to climb the 12,000 feet into a clear blue sky, and then the plane circled the landing area as the parachutists prepared for their jump.

Each tandem pair was attached at four points, connected at both shoulders and hips. They were to clear the plane and freefall for about 45 seconds before the instructor would pull the ripcord handle, to release the parachute which would open into a full canopy within a couple seconds. Three people jumped first, then Nikki with her instructor, and Jami with Terry followed.

The noise was deafening for Jami as the air rushed past, buffeting his body. He felt as if he could hear his blood coursing through his veins. Once the initial shock of falling through the air ebbed away, instincts took over. With his limited vision, Jami began to appreciate the beauty of floating. It was both exhilarating and calming. He'd never been in such a strong wind, yet knowing Nikki and he were having this experience together made him happy.

The time spent skydiving went by too quickly and the next thing Jami felt was the parachute opening with an upward tug, as air filled the orange, rectangular canopy. The gentle fall to Earth seemed anticlimactic compared to the initial freefall, but the slow descent under the parachute allowed time to appreciate the exciting experience. Although he couldn't see it well, he was sure Nikki's view was spectacular. Once on the ground, Jami was exhilarated—pumped. Grinning, he gave a loud, "*Yahoo!*"

When freed of their harnesses, Jami and Nikki embraced. "Thank you," he said.

"No, Jami, thank you," Nikki said before kissing him on the lips. This was actually their first kiss, and it was sweet.

BLIND LOVE 001

After changing back into their regular clothes, Hannibal drove them to a nice restaurant with Dave and Leigh following behind in their vehicle. Hannibal declined when Jami invited him to join them.

"It wouldn't be proper. I'm your employee," he said stubbornly.

"Hannibal, you're more than an employee, you're my friend," Jami said.

"Thanks, Jami, but I'll be fine. Since Dave and Leigh are here, can they bring you home?"

With Hannibal gone, the two couples were seated in a booth. After the waiter took their drink orders and gave them menus, Dave wanted to hear Jami's feelings about skydiving.

"It was scary. Even though we'd taken the instructions, the real thing is so different. Then, I guess I felt the freedom of eagles floating on air currents when they're soaring. The fear left me and I enjoyed the ride. Terry was very encouraging, which helped a lot. After the chute opened, I felt like a feather making my way down to earth."

Then Dave and Leigh turned their attention to Nikki. By then, the waiter was at the table ready to take their food order. Glancing quickly at the menu everyone placed their order. The guys ordered steaks, Leigh ordered grilled salmon, and Nikki got the grilled shrimp.

After the meal, they had to walk as was Jami's custom. But they didn't mind.

By mid-May, Nikki felt so comfortable with Jami that her resolve not to be alone with a man had just about disappeared. She even accepted a business meeting from one of her business acquaintances. He was a nice man from Michigan. He owned property in Chicago, and Nikki was his "go-to" agent anytime he needed to make a purchase.

His name was Madison Hudson, divorced with children who attended college in Michigan. He was average-looking with dark hair, olive complexion because of his Italian ancestry. He and Nikki had often had lunches together but never dinner. He'd told her that he was getting into town late but needed to talk so dinner would be an option. Nikki agreed because she felt comfortable with him.

She met him at a quiet restaurant in a neighborhood unfamiliar to her. He was waiting when Nikki entered the establishment. Madison was dressed casually, slacks and a polo shirt. Nikki also was dressed in slacks, a blouse, minimal jewelry, and heels.

As they ate, Madison asked her about a couple of commercial buildings he'd checked on the internet.

"Nikki, you're looking very lovely tonight," Madison said before sipping his whiskey. He'd already had three and was now working on the fourth.

"Thanks, but Madison, what's going on with you? I've never seen you drink this much before."

"You haven't? Yes, I guess so but then we usually only have lunch. I'm depressed. My ex-wife and I are having some problems."

"I'm sorry to hear that. Let's order you some coffee and we'll just talk." Nikki got the waiter's attention and coffee for Madison.

He finished his fourth whiskey before drinking the coffee. He poured out his heart to Nikki. She listened patiently—after all, he was a friend as well as a client. After a while he excused himself to use the men's room.

While Nikki waited her phone vibrated, and she saw that it was Jami. She returned his text, explaining that she was with a client but she'd be leaving soon, and that she would call him when she got home.

Madison returned with a sheepish grin. "Sorry, let's go." He looked at the check and threw a few bills on the table that more than covered the total due, plus a sizable tip.

It had been raining most of the day, and it had started up again as they were leaving the restaurant.

"Did you drive?" Madison asked.

"No, I took a taxi."

"I'll take you home. With this weather, you won't find a taxi or an Uber this time of night. I've got a car, it's just around the corner. You wait here and I'll run and get it."

Soon, a white sedan pulled up to the curb, and he waved for her to jump in. He didn't ask her where she lived, he just began driving.

Nikki asked, "Madison, where are we going? I don't live this way."

"I thought it would be nice to watch the lightning over the lake. We'll just be gone a few minutes and then you can give me your address." He smiled as he looked at her from the corner of his eyes.

Nikki began to feel a knot forming in her stomach, but she tried not to panic. After all, this was a man she'd known for a couple of years. He wouldn't attempt to do anything to her.

BLIND LOVE 001

The rain was heavy, making the view through the windshield blurry and distorted. Madison was driving faster than he should, but Nikki was afraid to say much. She was just trying to figure a way out of this situation. He turned off of Lake Shore Drive and onto a frontage road that followed Lake Michigan. Madison turned the car so that the headlights aimed out toward the lake waters.

The waves splashed against the large rocks as the rain continued.

Madison turned off the motor, then he turned to face her. "Nikki, why haven't you ever flirted with me? I'm not a bad-looking guy, and I've got plenty of money."

Nikki was taken aback. She really didn't know how to answer him. "I…I guess, I've never—I've never thought of you that way," She stammered, "I've considered you a friend and business associate." Nikki leaned against her door. She needed to get out of her seat belt first.

Madison leaned in closer, "Why not? Other agents I've worked with found me not such a bad guy. You're one of the prettiest, and you've never picked up on any of my signals. I like you, Nikki, and I can make your life so much better." Then he moved quickly, putting one hand between her thighs as his lips found hers.

Making a fist Nikki punched him in the eye as hard as she could. Releasing her seat belt, Nikki got out of the car after grabbing her purse. She didn't know which way to go but she knew that she had to get away.

As she ran, she saw a pedestrian bridge over Lake Shore Drive, and she headed in that direction. At the bridge, she got her phone from her purse and phoned her friend.

"*Jami!*"

Jami knew immediately from the sound of her voice that she was in trouble. "Where are you?" he shouted into the phone.

"I'm not sure. It's raining and I feel like an idiot."

"Look around, Nikki. You know the city. What looks familiar? Hannibal and I are on the way."

Jami yelled for Hannibal to get the car immediately. "What's going on?" Hannibal asked. He'd been watching one of his favorite cooking shows on the small television in the kitchen.

"It's Nikki. She's in trouble." Jami turned his attention back to Nikki. "Have you figured out where you are?"

"Hyde Park area. By the Museum of Science and Industry. I'm running across the pedestrian bridge. It's raining like crazy and I'm freezing. Oh, Jami, I'm such a fool."

"Is there a shelter where you can get out of the rain?"

"Yes, a bus stop across from the museum."

"Go there. We'll be there as quickly as we can."

Hannibal and Jami were in the car in minutes. Jami didn't know how fast Hannibal was driving but he knew that the speed limit was out of the question.

The traffic began to slow as they approached the intersection near the museum but once Hannibal made a right turn, he said, "Jami, she's here—she's sitting alone, kinda huddled over."

Hannibal slowed the car, and Jami opened the back passenger door as the car stopped. As soon as Nikki jumped in, Jami wrapped her in his arms. She was shivering.

"Hannibal, crank up the heat. She's freezing." Jami stroked her hair from her forehead. He released his hold on her to take his jacket off and wrap it around her. Then he took her in his arms again. Nikki was sobbing quietly while Jami just held her and didn't say a word for a while.

"Are you alright? Are you hurt?" Jami asked in a calm voice that hid his true anger. He needed information. "Can you tell me exactly what happened?"

Nikki didn't respond immediately. She shivered again, then sighing, she sat up to look at him.

"I'm not hurt, just mad and embarrassed."

"Who were you with?"

"One of my clients. His name is Madison Hudson. I've listed and sold various properties for him for a number of years." Nikki spoke in a quiet voice. She began to relate all that had happened. "Now I just want to go home, take a warm shower, and forget this ever happened."

Jami negated that idea. "You're coming home with me."

"Jami, I'm soaked and I don't have any clothes to change into."

"I understand, but my mother has some clothes at my place, and you're about the same size. I'd feel better if you stayed with me tonight. We'll get you home tomorrow. Hannibal will wash and dry your things, and you'll be all set."

Nikki was frowning. She was soaked and obviously exhausted. Finally, she agreed.

Hannibal stopped the car in front of the house. Jami's home was a three-story, gray-stone building with a separate entrance to the English basement. Jami wouldn't allow Nikki to walk. Instead, he carried her up the stairs to his front door. Hannibal unlocked and opened the door—the rain hadn't let up.

Max came to greet his owner as Jami walked toward the stairs without letting Nikki's feet touch the floor.

Hannibal watched as Jami made his way through the foyer and to the stairs. He then closed the front door and headed out to put the car in the garage.

"Jami, I'm fine, really I am."

Jami said nothing. His heart and mind were at war. He'd never experienced so much fear and anger in his life. Even with the loss of his vision, he'd felt nothing as he'd felt when he heard Nikki's voice. Then he realized that she'd phoned *him*, that she looked to *him* for protection.

After taking her into the second-floor guest bedroom he let her stand, but he held her close.

He kissed her. At first gently, then with more passion. She responded in kind.

"I'm sorry, it's just…." He couldn't finish his sentence.

"Don't apologize. I'm feeling the same way. This is very confusing."

He was still holding her close. Water dripped from her wet clothes but neither of them seemed to care about that.

"Nikki, I've fallen in love with you. I didn't realize it until tonight. When I thought you were in danger, I felt afraid. Afraid that I wouldn't have you in my life, and that would have killed me." He hugged her even closer.

Nikki sighed, being in his arms felt as if she belonged there. When did it happen? When did her feelings change from like to love? It had been so gradual. Their dates weren't just dates, hanging out together. Talking over the phone for hours at a time. Having their after-dinner walks. With him coming to her place and then walking together with Max seemed natural—normal.

Nikki shivered, "Jami, I need to get out of these wet clothes."

"Yes, of course. My mother's clothes are in the closet, and she has pajamas in the dresser drawers. I'll be in the kitchen waiting."

Once in the kitchen, Jami asked Hannibal if he knew anyone in the Detroit area.

"What are you thinking, Jami?"

"Madison Hudson tried to attack Nikki. He needs to be taught a lesson."

"Jami, I can see that you're really upset. I'll tell you what. We'll just cool off for the night, and tomorrow I'll make some calls. You need to think over what you're saying. Ms. Townsend seems to be able to take care of herself. I think this guy will rethink before trying anything with Nikki or any woman again," Hannibal said, before patting Jami on the shoulder.

Jami inhaled deeply as he rubbed his palms together. "I guess you're right. It just makes me angry when a man tries to force himself on a woman. If men would just realize that by making a woman feel safe, he'd have a better chance of having a good relationship."

Just then Nikki walked into the kitchen. She was wearing a too-large robe over a long nightgown. "That shower was the best. And Jami, unless your mother likes really large clothes, this is the smallest I could find."

Hannibal chuckled because it was obvious everything was too large. The belt of the robe was the only thing holding the nightwear in place.

Jami held out his hand toward the sound of her voice. "I'm sorry, I guess I'm not the best judge of women's sizes. And maybe these are the things my mother left here after she'd lost so much weight."

Nikki took his hand and he pulled her close. "Hannibal made you some tea to help you relax."

"Hannibal, do I look that silly?" Nikki asked as she adjusted the shoulders of the robe which kept slipping down. Hannibal nodded yes.

"Jami, Hannibal is smirking because these clothes are a little big." Nikki was trying to sound serious but she knew she did look clownish. Her hair was wild with crazy curls and no make-up.

"It's alright. It doesn't bother me," Jami said before kissing her cheek.

Then it dawned on Nikki that she could look sloppy and it wouldn't bother Jami because he couldn't see her.

"Here's your tea, it's chamomile to help you get a good night's sleep," Hannibal said as he slowly pushed the large cup toward her.

"Thanks, Hannibal." Nikki picked up the cup and began sipping the delicious warm drink.

They talked for a few more minutes until Nikki excused herself. She said she was tired and wanted to sleep. Jami walked with her to the bottom of the stairs. As she began to ascend, Jami didn't let go of her hand.

"Nikki, I meant what I said. I'm in love with you."

"Jami, I'm in love with *you*, too. But as happy as I am, I'm also so sleepy that I can't think straight."

"Okay, we'll talk more, tomorrow." He kissed her gently on her lips.

Early the next morning, Nikki awoke, and at first, she didn't remember where she was. Then, like an ocean wave, all memories of last night rushed into her mind—both the good and the bad. She felt angry with herself for not listening to her instincts. She shouldn't have gotten into the car with Madison. Even having dinner with him without someone else with her was a mistake.

Sighing, Nikki got out of bed. She'd slept well, that tea did its job. Nikki heard Jami and Hannibal's voices but couldn't understand what they were saying. Her clothes were laid out on a chair freshly cleaned and pressed. Even her undergarments looked new. Nikki found unopened toiletries in the bathroom, and she used them. After getting dressed, she joined the men in the kitchen.

"Good morning, everyone," she said as she entered.

They both responded with smiles and words.

"Jami, aren't you dressed early for court?" Nikki asked.

"Nikki, it's almost 8:30, and I've got to be in court by 10:00. We were deciding whether or not I should take a taxi to the courthouse, so that when you woke up, Hannibal could drive you home."

"It's still so dark outside. I thought I'd gotten up early, but I guess not. I'm sorry."

"Yes, it's been raining all night, and it's supposed to do this all day. It's just gloomy out. But anyway, Hannibal made a smoothie for you, unless you prefer something else."

"No," Nikki said. "That's great, and I just need some water."

After handing Nikki the glass of water, Hannibal excused himself but not before reminding Jami that they needed to leave in twenty minutes.

"Are you feeling alright this morning?" Jami asked.

"Yes, I feel wonderful."

"Can I get a kiss?"

"Of course," Nikki said, not hesitating for a second. She kissed deeply as she wrapped her arms around his neck.

Jami pulled her in closer, relishing in the taste of her mouth. His hands moved down her hips.

Slowly, Jami pulled away as he took deep breaths. He was finding it difficult to control his emotions. "Nikki, we've got to talk. This is serious. Come here tonight for dinner—5 o'clock?"

"I'll be here," she said and paused. "These feelings that we're having—are we rushing into something?"

"Not for me," he said.

At 5 o'clock, Nikki rang Jami's doorbell. She'd been to his home on numerous occasions, usually whenever they were going for a walk or jog with Max. Sometimes he invited her over for a movie night and a meal. But this time, it was different. Their feelings for each other had changed from friendship to love.

Jami opened the door and stepped aside for her to enter but she didn't get very far before he'd gently grabbed her by the arm, pulling her close for a kiss. This was getting to be a habit that they both enjoyed.

"How was your day?" Jami asked as he slowly released her.

"To be honest, good and not so good," Nikki said with a sigh. "Madison Hudson called and spoke to my broker Natasha. He claimed that I've flirted with him off and on over the years. And then last night I invited him to dinner under false pretenses!"

BLIND LOVE 001

As they walked toward the living room, Nikki continued her story. "Natasha told me this after I'd called her. Thank goodness I'd got my side in first. He told her that I'd tried to seduce him but he was faithful to his ex-wife and he wanted to reconcile their relationship, so he resisted me." Nikki's voice was becoming more intense as she spoke.

"That butt-hole—if I saw him right now, I'd punch him in the other eye."

"Okay, so what did Natasha say or do?" Jami asked in his attorney's voice.

"Natasha told him that our agency hated to lose his business but that I was too valuable. She also said that she would put the word out to all female agents not to work with him. She didn't want his possible reconciliation to be jeopardized...that he should only work with male agents." Nikki smiled. "I just love my broker."

"That's a smart woman," Jami said. "I've got to meet her."

"Yes, you must. And so, after that, my day was great. Now it's your turn. How's your case going?"

"I did my closing argument and now it's in the jury's hands. But I feel confident that we'll win—and if not a win, then maybe a reduced sentence."

As they walked hand in hand to the living room, Jami listened as Nikki shared her feelings from last night. She was still beating herself up about being blind to the obvious signals and red flags. "Why am I like that?"

"Nikki, you need to stop. You are human, and I'm sure many men and women have been suckered in by people like this Madison character. Besides, he's probably regretting that he ever tried anything with you. I would just like to know how he's going to explain his bruised eye."

"He'll probably lie." Nikki chuckled.

Sitting down on the sofa Jami put his arm around Nikki's shoulders, pulling her closer. "Now, how many houses did you sell?"

Nikki turned to look at him, then she smiled. "You're changing the subject."

"Yes, I am. I want you to let go of this anger. I can see why you're upset and you are right to feel the way you do. Honestly, I was so angry I considered doing bodily harm to that Madison character. But I need to talk to you about something more important."

Nikki sighed. She knew that he was right. She shouldn't let one near tragic mistake ruin an evening with the man she loved. However, she felt special when Jami said that he was also angry.

"Okay, what do you want us to talk about?"

"First, we have to go out to the back porch. Hannibal has made us a great dinner."

It was a mild evening with the sun low in the western sky. The shadows of the surrounding buildings looked like black uneven graphs crawling upward over the rooftops.

Stepping out onto the porch, she saw that small lights were wrapped around the railings. Candles in hurricane holders were on the floor. The small table was covered with a white lace tablecloth under clear glass plates. Two white wicker chairs with floral cushions were positioned opposite each other. Soft classical music played that seemed to eliminate the sounds of the city. A small bouquet of miniature pink and red roses was the centerpiece.

"This is beautiful!" Nikki said as she approached the table.

After she sat down, Hannibal seemed to appear out of nowhere. He carried a platter with broiled fish filets. There was also spinach salad, warm rolls, and wine. Nikki didn't realize how hungry she was until she began eating. Everything was delicious and then Hannibal brought dessert. He'd made chocolate cupcakes with chocolate chips in the chocolate icing.

"Hannibal, this is too much," Jami said as he reached for a second cupcake.

Nikki could only lean back in her chair. That meal had been perfect. "Hannibal, this was so good. Thank you so much. You're a master in the kitchen."

Hannibal, always a man of few words, smiled. "Thank you. Now I'll leave you alone. If you want anything else just call me."

Soft music began playing in the background. Jami stood up and reached out to Nikki, "Let's dance," he said. Nikki seemed to float into his arms. They moved effortlessly, enjoying the closeness of each other.

When the song finished, Jami wouldn't let her go. Nikki didn't mind, she liked having him close. "Nikki, I need to ask you something so let's sit down."

Nikki sat while Jami pulled his chair closer to her, then he took his seat. "I love you," he said,

"Oh, Jami, I love you, too."

"Are you sure? I know it sounds strange but when you said it last night, I was afraid it was just because of what had happened."

"No, it wasn't. I can't really say how long I've loved you, but I do."

"Then will you be my wife and marry me as soon as possible?"

Tears sprang from Nikki's eyes, "Yes, yes oh my goodness, yes." She hugged and kissed his cheeks and lips. They both were laughing and crying at the same time.

"Wait, I've got something," Jami said as he tried separating himself from Nikki. He reached into his pants pocket, pulling out a ring box. He handed it to her. "Open it," he said.

Nikki's hands were shaking. As she opened the box, a pear-shaped diamond greeted her gaze.

"Oh, Jami!" Nikki was breathless.

"Do you like it? I wasn't sure if you'd like a pear shape or square cut."

"To be honest, I don't need an engagement ring at all. Just a wedding ring would do me just fine."

"Really? Then I'll just return it," he teased.

"Nope, It's too late. I've got it on my finger and that's where it will stay until another ring replaces it. My wedding band."

They kissed again.

Standing, Jami held her close. He'd never thought a woman like Nikki would be his wife. She was not only lovely inside and out but an intelligent businesswoman as well. He really looked forward to the time they would be husband and wife.

"Jami, I don't mind spending the night tonight." Nikki's voice was so soft and alluring.

Jami smiled. "Please don't tempt me. But unless we're flying to Vegas tonight to get married, I'm still determined to wait until we're official."

"Are you sure? No one waits anymore."

"I know," Jami answered, "and I'm sounding crazy, but I've thought about this a long time. I guess I'm a romantic, and I want our first time to be special and not lust in the dust. Believe me, this is hard, but just as you're so special to me, I want our first time to be special by us being husband and wife. Because when I marry you, it will be forever. I'll never be with anyone else."

Nikki didn't know how to respond. Although she'd only been with one other man, she knew that Jami was her one and only. But waiting until marriage seemed so old-fashioned. She also knew that he'd been with other women because as their relationship grew, he shared with her things about some of his failed relationships. Maybe that's why he was being more cautious.

"Jami, if that's how you feel, I'm willing to wait. The more I think about it, the anticipation will be fun. So, I guess you're going to smother me with gifts and take me out for romantic meals. Since we're waiting, I expect to be a priority in your life. Is that asking too much?" Nikki said laughing.

"Not at all. Whatever you want, I'll do my best to give it to you. All I ask is your love and faithfulness."

"Jamison Bledsoe, you've already got my love. I really don't want anything from you except that you love me as much in return."

After many hugs and kisses, Jami decided that Nikki needed to get home. Hannibal drove the newly engaged couple to Nikki's apartment building. They'd decided that each would phone their respective parents and their friends the next day. And then they'd have dinner that night, Nikki wanted to cook a meal for Jami.

Saturday morning Nikki returned from her morning jog, showered, and then called her mother. As she waited for her to answer, Nikki couldn't stop admiring her ring. It was a lovely diamond set on a white gold band. "Hello, Mom," Nikki said when her mother finally answered. "I've got great news! Jami proposed to me last night!"

"What! He proposed, and I guess you accepted?"

"Of course, I'm in love. He's the very best man."

"Are you pregnant?"

"No, Mom—why would you ask that?" Nikki said, trying not to sound annoyed.

"Because he's blind, and you're too beautiful to be with a blind man. He can't appreciate how lovely you are, that's why. Nikki, how can a man like him enjoy being with a beautiful woman?"

Nikki took a very deep breath before responding to her mother's words. "Mom, Jami sees me better than any other man could ever see me. He sees me for the woman I am and not just some trophy to have on his arm. He loves *me* for *me*, and not just for my looks. And Mom whether you like it or not he is going to be your son-in-law. Now, I'm hanging up before you say anything else that could hurt my feelings." Nikki disconnected quickly and called her father. He'd be at work at his car dealership.

"Dad, Jami proposed last night!"

"Well, it's about time. So, when will I meet my future son-in-law?"

"I would like for you and mom to meet him sometime this week but your wife isn't keen on me marrying someone who is blind."

"Are you kidding me? Oh, that's why she's calling me now. Don't you worry, I'll take care of your mother. You come, say Thursday night for dinner. I'm looking forward to meeting this attorney who has won my only daughter's heart."

"Dad you're the best, but what about Mom? "

"I've got this. Don't you worry."

After a few more words, Nikki's Dad made her feel much better. Her parents had been married almost fifty years, and her mother was a handful, but Thomas Townsend had maintained his cool with his hot-headed wife. MariAnn was a mess but she loved Thomas and that was the glue that kept their marriage strong.

Nikki's father owned an automobile dealership and was quite successful, which allowed her mother to be a stay-at-home wife. Her mother's volunteer activities kept her busy as did Nikki and her two brothers. Nikki's older brother, Delbert, now worked with their father and her younger brother, Lawson, who lived in New Mexico, taught political science at college level.

Their father insisted that each year as the children grew up, they had to travel and visit one state every summer. Thomas Townsend didn't want his children to be ignorant or narrow-minded about their country. That was tradition until Lawson finished college. Then it stopped because Lawson moved to New Mexico, and Delbert's new wife only wanted to go overseas.

Now, Thomas and MariAnn traveled with their friends. Once a year, they had a big party for the extended family. Usually, that event was in early fall. Nikki loved her family and hoped that her mother would change her mind about Jami.

BENNA ELSE

Jami phoned his parents late Saturday morning with the news. Although they expressed joy that he was getting married, they wondered what type of woman would want to be with a man who was losing his sight. Was she after his money?

Jami was wealthy having received a trust from his paternal grandfather. Plus, being a very successful criminal attorney made him a very good catch.

"Son, you really haven't been dating that long. Isn't this a quick decision?" Jami's father James asked.

"Listen Pops, I'm not a teenager or a twenty-something asking for your permission. I'm just letting you know that I'm getting married. And it would be nice if my parents were at my wedding."

"Of course we'll be at your wedding. But we'd like to at least meet her first."

"Well, yes of course. What are you two doing next weekend?"

"Let me check, hold on." There were muffled sounds of conversation. "Okay, your mother said next Sunday would be good. I'm putting you on speaker. Now please tell us something about this woman who will be part of our family."

Jami couldn't stop once he began telling his parents about Nikki. He was honest in saying that she'd changed his life. He also spoke of how she had helped him go bike riding and learn to play golf. "She's added so much more to my life. She treats me as if I have complete vision. She is so patient and laughs with me and not at me if I make a mistake. I hadn't realized how safe I was making my life until she came into it. Now I'm jogging with her out in the park and we're visiting museums. Folks, she's the best thing that could have happened to me."

When Jami finally finished talking to his parents, he phoned Dave with the news. "Wow, I wondered how long it would take you to pop the question," his best friend said.

Jami asked, "When did you suspect that I would *pop the question?*"

"When you two went for that walk together at my folks' picnic. There was something, I don't know exactly how to put it but you both seemed comfortable with each other. Then, when you told me that you were going to be hanging out together—well, I guessed it wouldn't be long and I was right. I even told Leigh that you'd propose sometime this year, but I'm surprised it was this soon. So have you set a date?"

"No, but I'm sure it'll be soon."

"I'm your best man, of course," Dave said with a chuckle.

The two friends talked for over an hour. Dave still couldn't believe that Jami was waiting to be intimate with Nikki. Jami had his reasons and he kept those to himself. Although he was finding it quite difficult not to be naked with his now fiancé. He knew that tonight being alone with her at dinner at her home would be a challenge. He hoped that Nikki wouldn't try to tempt him from keeping his resolve.

Nikki was a nervous wreck all day. After phoning all of her family and friends about her engagement she began to clean the house. She wanted everything to be perfect. Jami was legally blind and wouldn't notice anything messy or dirty, but she would know and that was the point. She treated him as if he could see which meant her home had to be pristine.

The planned dinner would be simple—broiled salmon, rice, broccoli sauteed in butter, dinner rolls, and for dessert, gelato. And of course, white wine.

Nikki dressed carefully wanting to be alluring and provocative. So, she wore wide-leg pants, with a matching crop top and her hair in a short ponytail. Large hoop earrings finished off her look.

The doorman buzzed her apartment at 5:30, Jami was always on time. Nikki wondered if he waited outside if he were early just so that he'd be on the minute.

He had been to her home on several occasions but this time it would be different. They were more than friends now. Their relationship had changed and Nikki still couldn't believe that the man of her dreams would only see her as young. His vision would fade, and no matter how wrinkled she'd become he wouldn't see it. That was a wild thought.

The knock on her door brought her back. Nikki opened it, and Jami, looking confident and handsome, stepped inside. "Hello, beautiful," he said before taking her into his arms and kissing her. As usual, Max tried to get between the two lovers but to no avail.

The kiss was long but not long enough. Nikki felt dizzy when he finally released her.

"How are you feeling?" he asked, his voice deep and sultry.

"I'm…I'm okay." Nikki was breathless.

Jami laughed and hugged her again. "You're wonderful."

"Yes, I must agree with you," Nikki said with a giggle. "Well, come on in. Then looking down at Max she said, "You too, Max. You know you're always welcome," she said as she patted his head.

They walked hand in hand into her living room. Jami took a seat on the couch after releasing Max from his harness. Nikki went into the kitchen to get a vegetable tray with dip.

Once she sat down next to him, they talked about their day. He talked about his court cases and how he'd lost this case. Jami planned on appealing the verdict. He said that he had Hannibal doing a deeper investigation. "There's got to be a witness that we haven't found. I know in my gut my client is innocent," Jami said as he reached for a carrot stick on the tray.

"Hannibal can do that? He does some investigations for you?"

"Yes, he's pretty good. He's helped me on numerous occasions. This case is close to my heart. My client, Drake, is a young man who couldn't do it. It's just not in him."

"This sounds exciting. Isn't this the murder case where the police found that one fingerprint, and it was your client's print?"

"Yes, and he admits that he was at the murder victim's apartment. But he wanted to break up with her. He'd found out that she was seeing someone else. Drake says that she was alive when he left her."

"So, if you find a witness, then you can hopefully get a new trial?"

"Yes, that's the plan. You remember that other case with the young girl whose parents didn't have enough money to pay my fees?"

Since Nikki was sitting next to Jami, he could see her nod.

"Well, I just wanted you to know after winning her case, her parents moved out of their old neighborhood. She's attending a good school and even though her father has to drive farther to get to work, he's happy that his daughter is away from that bad element. And to answer your last question, if Hannibal finds that witness, we'll be good. But let's stop talking about this for now. These veggies are good, but I'm hungry and need food."

"Okay, I'm on it. Do you want some wine? The fish won't take long, and the rest of the meal is ready."

Nikki put the fish under the broiler and then brought Jami a glass of wine. He asked about her parent's response to their getting engaged.

BLIND LOVE 001

Nikki told him both her mother's reaction and then her father's. Jami listened without interrupting as was his habit. He focused on her face and her words.

"Nikki, you know your mother's concerns are honest. I can understand how she may be feeling." Jami said.

It didn't take long for the fish to broil and soon they were eating and having a lively conversation.

"Jami, my mother is a handful at times. She doesn't mince words with anyone. I'm surprised she has friends." Nikki said before taking a bite of fish.

"I'll be my charming self. After all, who can resist this smile?" Jami teased before laughing.

After dessert, they again sat on the couch, but Nikki sat away from Jami because she didn't want to renege on their agreement.

"Hey, why are you sitting so far away from me?" Jami asked. "I won't bite."

"Maybe you won't but I will. If I sit close to you, I can't guarantee my actions."

"You know I can contact my friend who will fly us to Vegas, and we can be married tonight."

Nikki didn't answer immediately, she was really thinking about his suggestion. She had a friend who had been married twice and both times in Vegas.

"Jami, I was thinking that September would be a perfect month for our wedding. Usually, the weather is nice—warm days and cool nights. I'd like to marry in my folk's backyard if that would be alright? And I'd like to keep it fairly small, maybe fifty to eighty people. What do you think?" Nikki asked.

"That's about two months away. Yes, I think we can hold out for two months—but no longer. Otherwise, we will be flying to Vegas."

"True, that! But I think we'd better double date for the next couple of months."

"Okay, but please come sit by me. I'll maintain control," Jami said as he patted the cushion close to him. Nikki slowly slid close and then placed her head on his shoulder.

Jami inhaled deeply, he loved the way she always smelled. "What is this signature fragrance you seem to always wear?"

"I'm glad you like it. There's a little fragrance and perfume shop in Old Towne. The owner makes custom fragrances for her clientele. So, my bath salts, lotions, and shower gel all have the same scent."

"Please never change it." He leaned down and kissed the tip of her nose. Soon, however, he was kissing her mouth. His hand slowly moved down to her hips as he shifted position. It happened so quickly but the tumble to the floor brought them both back to their senses. Somehow Nikki landed on top of Jami as they fell onto the wood floor.

"Ouch!" Jami exclaimed after hitting his head. Then he began laughing. "We're a mess," he said, still leaving his hands on Nikki's lower back and hips.

Nikki joined him in laughing as she nodded. Max, who'd been resting on the bed Nikki had purchased for him some weeks ago jumped to his feet. After trotting over to the couple, he put his nose in their faces with his tail wagging wildly. Which made them laugh even more.

Shooing Max away, Jami gradually rolled onto his side allowing Nikki to slide onto the floor next to him. Now they were face to face. "I am looking forward to making love to you," he said softly, "but you're right, we can't be left alone." Then he kissed her gently. Nikki snuggled close, as Jami searched in his pants pocket to find his phone. He called Hannibal, asking him to come and pick him up in fifteen to twenty minutes. Neither of them moved, they were enjoying being close.

After a few minutes, Jami said he needed to stand, and they both slowly got to their feet.

Nikki smoothed down her clothes as Jami also adjusted himself.

Max stood next to Jami as if he knew it was time to leave and Jami leaned down to stroke Max's head. The dog had slept almost the entire time since they'd arrived.

Nikki walked into the kitchen where she needed to breathe and compose herself. Jami came in right behind her. "Are you alright?" he asked.

"Jami, I love you so much it hurts. How is that possible? I was perfectly happy with my life before you and now I can't imagine my life without you." She had turned to him as she spoke.

BLIND LOVE 001

"I feel the same way. It's crazy, isn't it? But Nikki, you make my heart beat. Our love is blind. I will never love anyone the way I love you. You read books or see movies about this type of love, and I used to think, *oh, that's just a story*. But now I know it's real. Now I know that if anything happened to you, I couldn't live."

They hugged each other tightly as they both rocked slowly back and forth. "We're good together aren't we?" Nikki said.

"Yes."

The doorbell rang but Nikki was reluctant to leave Jami's embrace, though she finally did. She knew it was Hannibal and Jami had to go. She told the doorman that Jami was on his way down.

Nikki gave Max a pat on his head then she kissed Jami.

After closing the door behind Jami, she leaned back against it, she wrapped her arms around her chest, giving herself a hug. Then she smiled and whispered, "I need a cold shower."

CHAPTER 5

Wedding/Married Life

Two months went by quickly but smoothly. Dave and Leigh we're going to move into Nikki's condo after the wedding. It was just the size they needed. Leigh's new career as a wedding consultant was a plus for Nikki and Jami's plans. Leigh found the right caterers, photographer, plus an excellent videographer. Although the best wedding bakers were usually booked six months to a year in advance, Leigh explained the timeline to Ms. Charlotte, one of the finest bakers in Chicago. Telling Ms. Charlotte that *money was no object* finally persuaded her to make all of the pastries.

Jami and Nikki had to approve all the food and the cake. Nikki asked Jami if they could have cupcakes with different flavored centers and colorful frostings. She also thought the groom's cake could be cupcakes with shades of chocolate and creamy centers. She wanted cupcakes on a tier. Jami thought about the cupcakes for a couple of days. He tried to imagine what it would look like, being accustomed to the traditional wedding cake with the sheet cake for the groom.

BLIND LOVE 001

Since Nikki had her own ideas and he wanted to please his bride-to-be, he agreed. She asked him to select the flavors for the icings and the creamy fillings. So, Jami met with Leigh and Dave at the bakery. "This is your wedding also. I'm not getting married by myself. And I've selected the decorations, the colors. Don't you think you'll enjoy this?" He admitted he was looking forward to the taste testing.

Neither Jami nor Nikki wanted a bachelor or bachelorette party. Nikki went out with some of her co-workers and close friends for dinner. Earlier in the week, she had lunch with her mother and future mother-in-law at a swanky restaurant. Jami had his law partners, both dads, and Dave over to his house for bar-b-q, baked beans, coleslaw, potato salad, and beer. Hannibal prepared the meal. They played cards and watched the sports channel on television.

On the eve of their wedding, Nikki stayed at her parent's home in her old bedroom. It was fun being with just her parents one last time. They ordered Chinese food and reminisced about old times. From Nikki's school days to the beginning of her modeling career. Her dad recalled how, as a cheerleader, she fell and sprained her ankle and how it had scared him.

Nikki smiled as she lay in bed thinking how fast time flew by recalling the double dates with Phillie and Jonathan. She remembered the first words out of Phillipa's mouth, when meeting Jami were, "So you're the blind man that's won Nikki's heart." Then Jami smiled as he said, "Yes and I'm the only blind man who will always have her heart." They shook hands and became fast friends.

Nikki and Phillie first met at a runway show. Phillie was a tall blond with green eyes and a straightforward manner. They liked each other immediately and instantly became fast friends. Phillipa warned Nikki about Ron but Nikki wouldn't listen. Then, when Nikki first told Phillipa about Jami and his vision challenge, her first words were, "Girl, are you crazy? Why would you want to be with a man like that?" At the time she and Jami were just seeing each other as friends.

Nikki recalled how she and Jami were so wobbly on the tandem bicycle. She was in front with Jami maintaining his balance on the back seat. Nikki smiled thinking of the numerous times they fell and laughed as they got up. Thank goodness for knee and elbow pads, Nikki thought. She remembered sitting on the grassy slope across from Buckingham Fountain as they faced Lake Michigan. Jami could barely make out some of the sailboats, but he was enjoying hearing people talking as they walked past. "This is nice," Jami commented as he reclined on one elbow. "I never thought I'd ever ride a bike again. To be honest, I thought you were crazy when you suggested it." That had been one of their first dates.

Restless, Nikki sat up in bed. Sleep seemed impossible. Jami had changed her life for the better. His love was unconditional and he enjoyed just being with her. And she not only loved him but respected him. He was a man of integrity.

Nikki couldn't get to sleep thinking about her wedding. Her life would be so different. She was looking forward to being Jami's wife—and maybe having children in a couple of years. They really hadn't talked about that possibility. Laying back down and turning on her side, Nikki gazed out her bedroom window, wondering if Jami was as nervous as she was.

Hannibal," Jami called, "Have I forgotten anything?"

"No, Jami. I've got all your stuff for the honeymoon ready. Nikki gave me her suitcase a couple of days ago. It's all in the car. Dave's got the ring and you're all set," Hannibal replied, trying not to sound exasperated.

Hannibal couldn't help but smile to himself. He hadn't seen Jami this nervous since his first big murder case.

"Jami, everything will be fine. You and Nikki are the perfect couple. I'm fixing you some peppermint tea and a bagel. You need to eat something."

"I know you're right. I just don't want to mess up."

"The rehearsal went well, right? And the meal at the restaurant your parents reserved was excellent, wasn't it?'

"Yes, and yes. I guess I'm overreacting," Jami said as he sat down on one of the stools in the kitchen.

"We've got everything ready and, in a few hours, you're going to be a happily married man," Hannibal said, patting Jami's back.

"Hannibal, do you remember the conversation Nikki and I had about our honeymoon?" Jami said before biting into his bagel.

"You mean that ski trip? Yes, how can I forget? Nikki thinks you can do anything." Hannibal said. "She is some kind of woman, and she's just what you need. I'm happy that you two are going to be together. I can't wait to see you on skis."

"Yes, another sport to my growing list of things I thought I'd never be able to do. Her parents' cabin sounds nice. I may not be able to see everything but I'm sure she will describe what I can't see. She did say that there's a view from a cliff that is breathtaking. That's something I'll really be interested in."

"Yes," Hannibal said. "We'd better get some rest. Tomorrow will be a busy day."

Everything went off like clockwork and the day was beautiful. In a light breeze, scattered white clouds drifted across the bright blue Chicago sky. The Townsend backyard was a wonderful setting for the wedding. Colorful wildflowers lined both sides of the brick walkway. The gazebo was decorated with garlands of white, pink, and gray flowers. A tent occupied a section of the yard where the meals would be served and eaten.

The groom, best man, and the fathers wore gray suits with pale pink shirts and gray and pink ties. Nikki wanted to wear something comfortable and yet alluring. She chose floor-length slip dresses for both her and Phillipa. Phillipa's dress was a rose-pink color with a cowl neckline. Nikki's dress was a pale pink with a scoop neckline, and Connie had sewn miniature flowers on the straps. Both women carried two white lilies with Nikki having a pink rose with her lilies. The flowers were tied with a dark pink ribbon.

Since it was a small wedding, Jami and Nikki only had a best man and a matron of honor. They wanted it simple but elegant. The mothers wore shades of pink, while Max sat next to Jami with a pink and gray dog collar with a matching bow tie.

After their kiss as husband and wife, the guests stood and applauded as the bride and groom made their way toward the porch. As the guests went through the receiving line, the caterers rearranged the chairs. When guests left the line, they could get their food from the buffet and then find their seats.

It was a relatively small wedding with only seventy-five people in attendance. Each guest received a small bottle of champagne with Nikki and Jami's name and their wedding date on the label. The music began, and people ate, danced, laughed, and enjoyed themselves.

Two hours later, Jami whispered into Nikki's ear, "Have we thanked everyone?"

"Yes," she whispered back. They were dancing once again after having danced with every member of their respective families.

"Then we need to go," Jami said.

"Okay, but we should say a general farewell before we escape. So, let's make our way to the microphone on the gazebo."

Jami held Nikki's arm as they ascended the two steps up to the platform of the gazebo. Dave knew what was coming next so he quickly hurried toward the couple to adjust the microphone.

"Attention everyone. Jami and Nikki have something they want to say," Dave said before handing the mic to Jami.

"Nikki and I are so very happy that our family and close friends were able to be with us on our special day. I especially would like to thank Mr. & Mrs. Townsend for allowing us to use their beautiful home for our wedding. All of you have given us a fantastic beginning to our life together. Now, I think Nikki wants to say something." Jami then handed Nikki the mic.

"Jami pretty much said everything that I wanted to say. So please enjoy yourselves and thank you all again."

As they made their way down from the gazebo, white and pink flower petals began to fall around them. Nikki and Jami went through the house and exited out the front door. Both sets of parents were there, and they hugged each other once again. Hannibal and Max were waiting by the car.

Nikki was surprised at Hannibal's timing. After getting settled in the backseat Nikki asked, "Hannibal, how did you know when we were leaving?"

"Jami signaled me."

"How?"

"His phone. He just told me when I call you that means we're leaving. So have the car and Max ready."

BLIND LOVE 001

Nikki looked at Jami who had a smug expression on his face. Nikki had to laugh. "I love you, Jamison Bledsoe," Nikki said before kissing him deeply.

They didn't plan a regular honeymoon because both had job commitments. Nikki had a closing that she just couldn't miss, and Jami desperately wanted to see the trial through to the end. So, they just took a week off of work and stayed in Chicago. Their real honeymoon was planned for spring when they'd go spring snow skiing.

They arrived at the Ritz Carlton Hotel on Michigan Avenue, said goodbye to Hannibal and Max, and checked in. The bellman took them up to their suite.

"I didn't think this day would ever come," Jami said before sweeping Nikki up into his arms. "Now guide me to the bedroom. I don't want to trip over a chair and drop you."

Nikki navigated their way to the bedroom. Once by the bed, Jami let her down to stand up.

"Now please turn around so I can unzip this lovely dress." His voice was soft and quiet.

Nikki complied. Her heart was racing, and she could barely breathe. The dress fell softly to the floor around her feet. Jami hugged her before she could turn to face him. He began kissing her shoulder and neck. Nikki went weak, she'd waited so long for this, her legs felt like noodles, and she would have collapsed if he hadn't been holding her.

Nikki moaned softly and that's when he picked her up again and placed her gently onto the bed.

"I'll make love to you, my love," he said as he took off his jacket, removed his tie, and began to unbutton his shirt. "I want to memorize every inch of your body. I want you to know the joy of being loved by a man who is completely committed to your feelings."

◈

When Nikki awoke the next morning, Jami was still asleep with his arms wrapped around her. Her head was on his shoulder as she watched his chest move up and down. They had made love numerous times. It seemed they couldn't get enough of each other. Nikki smiled thinking of their lovemaking. They laughed and they tickled each other. They had enjoyed a gift from the hotel—a bottle of pink champagne with fresh strawberries. Sometime during the night, they'd called for room service because neither of them had eaten much at the wedding.

They didn't leave their suite until the following morning. They walked down Michigan Avenue over to Oak Street Beach. It was a cloudy day but they didn't care. Life was good and they had each other. Without Max, Jami used his cane and when Nikki paused at a shop window, she told Jami what it was she was looking at. "Do you want to go inside to buy something?" he'd asked.

"Nope, I've got everything I need. I just like to look sometimes."

Then they walked through the pedestrian walkway underneath Lake Shore Drive. They ambled west on Oak Street, which featured numerous boutiques. Nikki often purchased her outfits in these shops. Her favorite shop's window had an outfit that caused her to let out a little gasp.

"Okay, what did you see?" Jami asked. He knew something had caught her eye.

"Oh, my goodness. It's just too perfect but I really don't need it," Nikki answered as she studied the lines of the dress.

"Why don't we go in and you can try it on. After all, this is our first honeymoon. If we were in Europe or some other foreign land, you'd be buying clothing."

"You're right," Nikki said, and she led him inside the store.

She found a chair for Jami and told the sales associate that she wanted to try on the dress in the window. It was a fall dress with long sleeves, shawl collar, fitted bodice, and a straight skirt. It fit perfectly.

Nikki approached Jami, "Okay, my dear husband, feel this dress on me," Nikki said.

"Really?"

"Yes, because it's gorgeous and fits me, but I want you to see it."

"Can I see it in the fitting room?" Jami asked with a smile.

"Yes, come with me," Nikki said as she grabbed his hand, pulling him out of the chair.

When they got into the dressing room, Jami's hands moved all over Nikki's body.

"Yes, I like it," he said in a very deep and sensual voice. "Now hurry, take it off, buy it and we can get back to our suite. You're killing me, woman." Then he pressed her body against the wall of the dressing room, kissing her deeply. "Hurry up," he said before leaving her.

Nikki dressed quickly, and by the time she was out of the dressing room, Jami had paid for the dress.

"You know we're crazy," Jami said.

"Yes, isn't it fun sometimes?"

It was now the middle of October, and the weather was mild for Chicago. The days were sunny and warm but the evenings were getting cooler. Jami, Nikki, Max, and Hannibal got into a comfortable routine. During the week, everyone was up early to exercise. Usually, Jami and Nikki jogged with Max and Hannibal was in his routine of working out in the basement gym.

About an hour later, breakfast would be served—then it was showers and getting dressed for work. Sometimes Nikki didn't have to go into her office until later in the morning. However, Jami always left the house by eight-thirty. Hannibal took Jami either to his office or to the courthouse. Max was always with Jami which left Nikki alone in the mornings. Hannibal usually did errands like getting fresh produce, going to the dry cleaners or sometimes Jami had him helping with a case.

In the evenings, Jami tried to be home by five but sometimes he had to return to his office to meet with a client. Once in a while, Nikki had to show a house or a property in the evening. But Hannibal always stayed flexible with their meals, making sure that all were as healthy and organic as possible. Friday night was date night, and Nikki and Jami always went out. No matter what, they made that night theirs. They'd attend a movie or they would go to a play or a concert. Sometimes they'd be with their friends and other times it was just the two of them.

One evening as they strolled along Clark Street, Jami asked Nikki a question that surprised her.

"Babe, if something should happen to me, would you remarry?"

"Jami, why would you ask such a question? Are you alright? There's nothing wrong with you, is there? Nikki was fearful.

"No, I'm fine. I just wondered. You're so beautiful and yet you love me so much. I don't want you to be alone. And you would be very wealthy if something should happen to me, you know."

"Jami Bledsoe, you are talking about something very strange. What happened today? You're bringing up a horrible subject."

Jami sighed and said, "One of my law partner's brothers died suddenly and he was my age. He was healthy but he had an aneurysm. I guess it just kind of flipped me out. He was married with children, and I thought about us. That's all."

Nikki stopped in her tracks which caused Jami to stop too. She got in front of him and looked up into his face. "Jami, first of all, I love you so much. And second of all, nothing in this life is guaranteed. We must take each day as it comes. But knowing this, I could never be with another man. I'll just grow old alone with the memories that we make each day. To be honest, I started a diary because I want to be able to recall most everything we do. And if something happens to either one of us, we'll have my journal. Would that be alright?"

The tension seemed to ebb from his body as he hugged tightly. "Yes, thanks, I needed to hear that."

After the hug, Nikki stepped back and punched him hard in the stomach. "*Hey!*" Jami shouted.

"I never want to hear you talk like that again! You are not going to leave me, do you understand?" It troubled Nikki to even consider that Jami wouldn't be with her forever.

"I'm sorry, but that punch wasn't fair. You know I couldn't see it coming," Jami said, rubbing his stomach. He was glad that he wasn't soft in the midsection. "You're pretty strong for a skinny woman," he teased. He then reached out to pull her in close. "I really do apologize."

"Well, okay, but please don't say things like that to me. You made my heart hurt," Nikki said as she rested her head on his chest.

Slowly they resumed their walk, headed for home.

The following evening, they went to a party. Nikki drove since Hannibal had the night off. Max stayed home alone. One of Jami's law partners and his wife were celebrating their anniversary. Jami wanted Nikki to wear the purple dress he'd purchased from the boutique.

When they arrived, vehicles were parked in the driveway and on the street. They had valet parking, but when a young man approached them to say he'd take care of their car, Nikki was reluctant. But Jami assured her it was okay. He'd been there before and his friend, Jack, always had valet parking for a large party.

Nikki and Jami entered the house which was buzzing with people. Jack immediately approached them. "Hey, guys, I was wondering when you'd get here," Jack said as his wife quickly joined him.

"Hello, Nikki," Anna, Jack's wife, said. "I haven't seen you since your wedding. How are you both?"

Jack took Jami's arm and led him around and introduced him to some of the guests. Anna took Nikki with her to converse with some of the women.

As the evening progressed, Nikki had the chance to make some business contacts and watch her husband socialize. Since their marriage, they'd stayed close to home just enjoying each other. So this was one of their first outings as husband and wife.

Jami was enjoying himself. Jack and Jami had been friends since law school, and they'd decided to eventually open their own firm as partners. Now they were successful and their firm had grown to include four additional attorneys. Their law office covered divorce, personal injury, and real estate law, and their reputation as an honest and reputable firm grew quickly in the Chicagoland area.

Music was playing on the enclosed patio as Nikki approached her husband, who was having a conversation with a couple of men.

"Excuse me, gentlemen, I must steal my husband away for a bit," Nikki said. Then she took his hand, leading him toward the music.

"I've missed you," Jami whispered into her ear when they began dancing. The music was smooth and soft. "I feel like we haven't really talked all night."

"We haven't. You've been busy talking to other attorneys and Anna has had me with the wives of the attorneys. Do you realize that most of those women don't work outside the home?"

"No, but I'm sure some do volunteer work."

Then he twirled her around before drawing her back into his arms. After their dance, they went to the buffet. Nikki told him what was available, and Jami made his selection. Nikki carried both plates and found an empty table. Once Jami was situated, she went to get drinks.

"Hello, pretty lady." A man came and stood next to her. "Can I help with your drinks?" he asked.

"No thanks. I think I can handle two glasses," Nikki said as she stepped away from him. She didn't remember seeing him earlier in the evening, and she wondered where he came from. She didn't like the way he looked at her and she felt his stare as she walked back to Jami.

As they ate, Nikki glanced around and saw the stranger staring at her. She felt uneasy but she wasn't going to allow him to mess up their evening. She turned her attention to Jami and began to ask him questions about the different people at the party.

After eating, they mingled with some of the other guests. It was getting late, and Nikki was tired. She asked Jami if he was ready to go home. Some of the guests had left already, and it was almost 11 o'clock.

Anna happened to see them looking around. "Hey, are you two ready to go home?" she asked.

"Yes," Nikki said. "This was really nice, but Jami and I get up early to go jogging."

"Jack and I should start doing something like that. I'll get your coats and find Jack. He'll want to say goodbye." As Anna walked away, the stranger approached them.

"Hey, Jami! How are you, ole man?"

"I'm great and you, Cole—how's life been treating you?" Jami asked.

Nikki noticed that even though he was speaking to Jami he kept his eyes on her. Nikki took Jami's hand as she moved closer to her husband.

"I heard you got married, and I'm guessing that this young lady here is your bride."

"Yes, and I know your reputation, Cole."

"Hey, now man. I just wanted to say hello and meet her. I'm looking to invest in some real estate and heard that she is one of the top agents in Chicago."

Jami's smile was more of a sneer. His instincts were on point. He knew Cole was a "player" who was always after another man's wife. Jami had heard how good-looking and smart he was. And he knew that Cole had been married twice to wealthy women. After each divorce, he ended up getting a substantial settlement.

"Who are you here with this evening?" Jami asked, knowing full well that he was with a middle-aged widow with plenty of money.

"Helen Jenkins. Do you know her?"

"Cole, stop looking at my wife and look at me. I really don't want to have an issue. My wife has a wicked right hook," Jami said.

Cole looked surprised and a little shocked. "You're kidding me!" he said.

"Don't try your luck," Jami said as he squeezed Nikki's hand gently.

Anna approached them with husband in tow and coats in hand.

With warm goodbyes to Anna and Jack and a cool nod toward Cole, Nikki and Jami left. After getting into their car, Nikki leaned over, giving Jami a kiss on his cheek. "How did you know about that Cole character?" Nikki asked as she started the car.

"I have eyes that are only for you," Jami said with a smile.

"No, really Jami, how?"

"Babe, don't get angry, but I knew when we got married there would be some men who think because I'm blind they can flirt with my wife without me knowing it. I trust you, but some of these men have only one thought. Jack is my good buddy. He told me that Cole was here, and he was checking out his next victim. Jack also saw him come up to you when you went to get our drinks.

"I could also tell when you sat down to eat, your voice gave you away. Nikki, I can tell your moods by the tone of your voice."

"Really?"

"Do you remember when I said how deep my love is for you? Nikki, I know you better than you know yourself. It's crazy but you're my girl."

"Jami, that's weird and comforting at the same time. I don't quite know how to respond to that."

"I don't want you to think I'm possessive. I just want you to know that I'll protect you anyway I can."

This conversation comforted Nikki. As they headed home, Jami changed the subject and talked about some of the people at the party. It took almost an hour to drive home, and Nikki was surprised that Jack commuted so far daily. Jami explained that Jack took a commuter train to get downtown then he'd get a taxi to the office. Most of the other attorneys lived in the city or just outside the city limits.

Max was happy to see them and Hannibal had texted Jami that Max had been walked and was good for the night.

Nikki and Jami made love in a caring and gentle kind of way. Nikki's joy was always foremost in Jami's heart and mind.

As the leaves of autumn continued to change from green to golden yellow and rusty red, and the wind off of Lake Michigan seemed to get stronger and colder. Jami's caseload mounted and he was working many evenings at the office. Nikki would take him an evening meal that Hannibal prepared and they'd eat at his desk. Jami's sister, Jonell, would join them sometimes but usually she would go out to get food for herself.

"Does your sister like me?" Nikki asked one evening while they were eating at the office.

"Yes, I guess. Why do you ask?"

"She sometimes seems very cool towards me. I've tried to be friendly. I've asked her on several occasions to join me and my friends when we do our Saturday luncheon."

"I can't really say. But perhaps she thought that I'd never marry. She pretty much dedicated herself to helping me. I've encouraged her to return to school and get a law degree but she won't." Jami paused for a moment. "When I found out that I would be blind, Jonell seemed to take the news harder than I did. I was an emotional mess. But she was always trying to encourage me. When my parents decided to pay for me to go on a trip around the world, she wanted to be with me. However, our father thought it best if Dave went with me instead. We were gone for a year and when we returned, she seemed different somehow."

"In what way?" Nikki asked.

"I think since I'm younger, she's always felt like she's needed to take care of me. Our parents have always been busy with their lives and Jonell, well she's just been there for me. When I decided to go into law, she began working in a law office and decided to become a law clerk. So, when Jack and I opened our office naturally, she was our first hire.

"I never thought I'd fall in love and get married and I think she thought the same. So perhaps she's a little jealous because you're in my life more than she is."

"Well that explains a lot," Nikki said. "I'll continue to be as friendly as I can toward her."

Jami nodded. "Yes, and I'll do my best to let her see that you truly make me very happy. But she's needed and loved by her little brother."

The following weekend Nikki, Jami, Hannibal, and Max were on their way to dinner at Jami's parents' home. Every year, Jami's parents went to Africa the third week in November and stayed until the first of the new year. James Bledsoe volunteered his time and skills at a clinic each year for a little over a month, and Jami's mother went with him.

"I think it's wonderful that your folks do that," Nikki said.

"Yes, it is. When my sister and I were younger, we went with them. It was great fun for us—no school, or at least not regular school. Our mother had us doing schoolwork and online schooling. I went until I graduated high school."

"What was it like to be there?"

"There was some poverty and that's where dad did most of his work. The clinic was always busy but when he got time off, we went on road trips. Seeing the wild animals and experiencing the beauty of that country was exciting."

"Maybe we could go there someday," Nikki said. "In all my travels I never made it to Africa."

"Then I guess we can add that to our bucket list."

Louise, Jami's parent's cook, had prepared a traditional Thanksgiving meal and, as usual, everything was delicious. Jami could not stop praising her cooking.

Jami's father told them, "Jami and Nikki, thanks for coming tonight. And Nikki, we'd just like to say how happy we are that you're in our family,"

"Oh, thank you, James," Nikki answered, a little embarrassed but pleased by his words.

He nodded to her. "I've got a daughter, but now I feel like I have *two* daughters, and it's a good feeling. We've never seen Jami happier and to be honest, I didn't think it would ever happen. Since we won't be here for Christmas, Nikki, I have a gift for you."

With a smile, Jami's mother, Leah, handed Nikki an elongated black box. "We hope you like it."

Nikki slowly opened the box to find a gorgeous diamond and emerald bracelet. Nikki gasped. "Oh, my." Lifting the narrow bracelet from its case, tears came to Nikki's eyes as she looked up from the bracelet to her in-laws. Nikki had not felt truly welcomed. This surprise gesture spoke to her saying she was indeed part of the family.

"Thank you, thank you so much! Jami, look at this!" she said, turning to her husband. She put it in his hands, and he held it close to his eyes to see as much of it as he could. Then smiling, he gave it back to Nikki. Nikki hugged her in-laws while thanking them again.

She had Jami clasp the bracelet of square cut emeralds edged with round diamonds.

"Jami, did you know about this?" Nikki asked.

He shook his head.

His mother, Leah, said, "We wanted to get *you* something, Jami, but you've got just about everything a man would want. So, your dad went to a custom watchmaker and had him make a designer talking watch for you." Leah handed Jami his gift. It was a magnificent large round shape with an open face, so the inner workings of the watch were visible. "Wow!" was all Jami could say. He had Nikki place it on his wrist. They both admired the timepiece.

"We weren't expecting to exchange gifts. Otherwise, we would have gotten you two something," Nikki said.

"Normally we don't do gifts until we return from Africa. But because of you, Nikki, we wanted to make an exception. We're so happy that you're part of our family," Leah said and James nodded in agreement.

When they left his parent's home Nikki truly felt part of Jami's family. She knew it would take time to really get to know each other but this was a great beginning.

BLIND LOVE 001

As the days got shorter, Nikki and Jami remained in a honeymoon state of mind. One evening they were lounging in one of the former bedrooms on the second floor. Jami had converted this room into Nikki's home office. Jami sat on one end of the sofa with earbuds in, listening to an audio novel, while Nikki lay on the opposite end of the couch with socked feet on Jami's lap. With her head propped on pillows, she was reading a mystery novel.

"Yeah, Jami," Nikki said as she wiggled her feet to get Jami's attention. "Do you think we could teach Max to track us?"

He turned to face her. "Do you mean like the K-9 dog in that movie we watched the other night?"

"Exactly," Nikki said. "I think it would be a fun game. And Max would learn a new skill."

"So, it's not enough that he's already my service dog," Jami teased.

"Max is so smart. We could each take turns hiding someplace here in the house. I could take him out onto the back porch, and you go and hide. Then, when I think you've hidden, I'll give Max the command '*Find Jami!*'"

Max, who'd been laying by Jami's feet, perked up his ears upon hearing his name the first time. He was now watching the back-and-forth conversation.

Nikki watched her husband as he considered her idea.

"Okay, why not. It might be fun. When do you want to start?"

"Tomorrow night. And when he finds either of us we'll give him a treat and lots of hugs."

So the training began. The two of them took turns taking Max out of the house while the other one hid. The command *Go Find Jami* or *Go find Nikki* took a while but after three weeks of daily training, Max got it. He even made a different whimper for Jami and Nikki.

Hannibal had watched in amazement as Max would scurry around the house seeking whichever one was hiding.

The first week in December was unusual for them. Jami's murder case was still in the works. Hannibal had been trying for weeks to find a witness. Finally, he knocked once again on the door across the hall from the murder victim's apartment. No one had answered on previous attempts. This time, a dog barked, then he heard a woman's voice asking who he was.

"Hello, my name is Hannibal Jackson. I work for attorney Jamison Bledsoe. He's defending the young man who was accused of killing the woman who lived across the hall from you." As the door opened Hannibal found himself looking down at a petite white-haired, blue-eyed woman. He handed her his card and she took it.

"Well, come in, don't just stand there," she said with a warm smile.

Hannibal was surprised that she showed no fear. After all, he was a tall man with an athletic build. But she didn't seem phased. She directed him to sit down in a wingback chair and she made herself comfortable in a recliner.

"My name is Mrs. Bertha Schloss, and this is Chili, my terrier and watchdog. So, you're working for the defense, is that correct?"

"Yes, and I've been looking for anyone who could help. We know our client didn't kill Ms. Ferguson, but since the police found his fingerprint, well, you probably know the story."

"I do, but I've been away visiting my daughter's family. I just returned home the day before yesterday. I don't know if I can be of any help."

"Mrs. Schloss, anything you could recall would be helpful. When did you leave town?"

The elderly woman tilted her head slightly. She was in deep thought for what seemed like several minutes. Then she said, "Wait, I do remember something. I'd finished packing and I was waiting for my ride. My friend Glenda was taking me to the airport. Glenda is very nice, she just drives so slowly. I'm surprised that she hasn't been in any accidents."

"Mrs. Schloss, please, could you continue?" Hannibal pleaded as he leaned forward in his chair.

"Oh, yes, sorry. So, as I was saying, I heard voices. So I looked out of my peephole and saw that young man leaving. He was angry and she said some horrible things to him before slamming her door."

"So, she was alive when he left? Great!" Hannibal said.

"Ahh, but there's more," Mrs. Schloss said, "About ten to fifteen minutes later I heard someone else banging on Vicki's door. Vicki was her first name. Anyway, it was another guy." Mrs. Schloss shook her head with a disgusted look on her face.

"What other guy?"

Mrs. Schloss leaned forward as if she had a secret that she wanted only Hannibal to hear. "This guy was a mess. I think he was on drugs. Whenever I encountered him in the hall, he expected me to move out of his way! The nerve of some people!"

"What did he look like?"

"He was under six feet tall with dirty blonde hair. His eyes were a light color, like gray or green maybe. He smelled of cigarettes or something worse. I didn't like him and he treated Vicki horribly. I'd hear him calling her terrible names but for some reason she took that abuse."

"Did he drive a car?"

"My goodness, yes. It had those spinners on the hubcaps. Oh yes, he had a vanity plate on the front. Now let me think, what did it say?" She paused again in deep thought.

Hannibal was beginning to get his hopes up. This was the break he and Jami had been hoping for.

"'Slick B' that's what it said." Mrs. Schloss beamed, proud that she remembered.

"Mrs. Schloss, would you be able to come to court with me tomorrow? Mr. Bledsoe would really like to speak with you. I would pick you up, or if you feel safer, you could have your friend drive you."

"If you think I could help, yes, I'll come."

"I have to ask you something. Why weren't you afraid of me when you opened the door?"

"You mean because you are a big chocolate man with broad shoulders and I'm a little old white woman?" She chuckled.

"Well, yes."

"You look like one of my sons. I adopted boys of color for many years. My husband and I loved kids. We had a total of seven children. Four adopted and three of our own, although they were *all* ours. You reminded me of Dwayne."

"And where is Dwayne now?"

"He's a doctor and lives in Oregon. I'm going to visit him next month."

When Hannibal left Mrs. Schloss, he called Jami to tell him the news. So, for Jami, it was a great week. He got his client off and the real killer was caught—a good, but unusual week

Nikki had a house showing in the late afternoon. The buyers wanted to look at the house for the second time. Nikki had tried to contact the owner to no avail. She finally decided to go to the house in hopes that the owner had gotten her voicemails not to be home between the hours of 4:00 and 6:00.

She arrived half an hour before the potential buyers were to meet her. The house was a nice brick single story with a full basement, remodeled kitchen and bathroom. Nikki first went to the kitchen and prepared a diffuser with essential oils with a citrus fragrance.

She walked about the house to make sure it was tidy. Unfortunately, when she got to the master bedroom, the owner was laying across the queen size bed face down with only a bath towel across his hips. Nikki gasped, then muttered expletives before approaching the sleeping man. At least she hoped he was sleeping and not drunk or dead.

"Mr. Groves, Mr. Groves, please wake up," Nikki said, as she tapped his shoulder.

Nothing.

"Mr. Groves," Nikki raised her voice and tapped him harder. He moved and groaned but didn't seem fully awake.

Nikki carried a whistle for emergencies. She got it out and stepped out of the bedroom because she didn't want to see something she shouldn't. Turning her back to the bedroom, she blew the whistle as hard as she could.

She heard him hit the floor. Then he yelled out a stream of profanities. "Mr. Groves, it's Nikki Townsend, your real estate agent. I've tried to contact you all day. There are people coming over to look at your house. I need you to be gone."

"What? Wait! How much time do I have?"

"Ten minutes."

"I'll do it. I broke my phone, and I haven't gotten any messages. Sorry, but I'll be gone in five minutes."

Mr. Groves' exit out the back door couldn't have been any closer. As soon as the back door closed, the front doorbell rang. Nikki composed herself, then greeted the potential buyers with her warmest smile.

The couple, both in their early fifties, were serious buyers. This was their second time looking at the residence. Nikki didn't speak much unless they asked her a question. She wanted them to feel comfortable as they went from one room to another. The husband had a tape measure and pad while his wife inspected the kitchen and looked closely at the back porch. She had a loom and sold tapestries and small rugs. Her husband worked with wood, making various small cabinets and shelving. They both loved the size of the backyard. It was, in their opinion, perfect for a garden.

It was getting late, Nikki was tired and finally they were ready to leave. They told Nikki how much they were willing to pay. It was a little under the asking price, but Nikki was sure Mr. Groves would be happy with the offer. His new job in Texas started in a month, and he needed to go.

By the time Nikki got home, all she wanted to do was get into her PJs and go to bed. When she walked inside the house, it was quiet. She made her way into the kitchen, and she found a note in Hannibal's handwriting, it said "Had to go out. Not an emergency, just some clients. Sandwich is for you."

Jami and Hannibal sat in the car with Max waiting for the "clients" to show up.

"Hannibal, are you positive they're meeting us?" Jami asked.

"Yes, Saul phoned me and said it was urgent. He's an old friend, and I feel I owe him. He helped keep me out of serious trouble. Until I met you, Jami, I was always running and hiding from the law."

"Yes," Jami recalled. "If I hadn't been your attorney, you would have been in jail for a long time. It was your third offense."

"You're an excellent lawyer."

"Thanks. Now tell me what Saul said, exactly?"

"Okay. There was a fight and someone was wounded. Saul's nephew was involved in the fight but he didn't have a weapon. Saul heard about the fight and got to the scene before the cops. He snatched his nephew, Willie, out of harm's way. But Willie wants to tell the truth about what happened. That's why he called me."

"Does Willie have a criminal record?"

"When he was a juvie. But he's really trying to stay out of trouble."

By then a large cream-colored SUV pulled in behind them. A man stepped out of the vehicle and came up to the driver's side to speak to

Hannibal. It was Saul, and he said Willie was in the SUV and was bleeding. He was the person who got shot.

"You mean to say," Jami interrupted Saul, "that Willie is bleeding in your car?" Why didn't you get him to a hospital?"

"Mr. Bledsoe, gunshot wounds and hospitals mean police. I wanted Willie to be represented by a lawyer. I've got him bandaged up real well."

Jami closed his eyes to think. "Okay, we're going to the nearest hospital. Just follow us. I'm going to phone a detective friend and have him meet us there. Then you and Willie can tell the story as to what happened and I'll be your attorney."

When Jami, Hannibal, and Max finally arrived home, it was well after midnight. While they were at the hospital Jami had taken the time to contact his wife.

Nikki ran down the stairs when she heard them coming in. She had dressed in a tracksuit because she didn't know if she would need to meet Jami somewhere and she didn't want to be in her pajamas.

"Jami, are you alright?" she said as she ran into his arms and hugged him. "Why didn't you text me instead of having Hannibal leave a note?"

"I was busy with an issue from my office and Hannibal prefers pen and paper. And yes, we're fine. I'll tell you all about it in the morning. I've talked myself to death tonight," he said as he returned her embrace. Then he told Hannibal that he wasn't going into the office until late tomorrow. "I need sleep."

Hannibal watched as the couple headed toward the stairway, with Max trailing behind them. He was proud of his friend tonight. Jami truly cared about people even if they weren't well-to-do.

Nikki's family had a huge Christmas gathering that Jami was reluctant to attend. He didn't want to be a bother and he felt he would be in the way. Usually, during the holidays, he was alone with Max. He gave Hannibal time off and Jonell would usually go on a cruise with friends. Jami's court cases were given continuances until after the first of the year. So, Jami cooked, took walks, read, and listened to the television. He was accustomed to the quiet and he had come to enjoy the solitude.

Nikki begged and pleaded for him to come with her until he gave in.

"I can't imagine not having you with me," she said.

"But Nikki, most of the men will be watching the games on television, and you'll probably be with your mother and the other women helping to prepare the food. I may as well be home," Jami reasoned.

"Jami, are you feeling sorry for yourself?" Nikki asked.

"Nope. I just know that some people feel uncomfortable being around someone with a disability. I want you to have fun with your relatives and not be concerned about me. I've been by myself for years and I don't want to be a burden for you."

Nikki understood his point of view but she didn't like it.

"Jami, I guess I'm being selfish."

Jami sighed. "Okay, I'll go—and you're not being selfish. You just don't think of me as having a disability. As normal as I try to be, my dear wife, some situations make me feel uncomfortable."

The event at the house wasn't a complete disaster. Jami and Max found a spot in the basement to listen to the football game. And Jami had a small radio so he could hear the play-by-play. Nikki checked on him now and then to make sure he was having a good time. Tom, Nikki's father, stayed close to Jami to make sure he was aware of everything that was going on around him.

Nikki and Jami had purposely arrived late because she knew that they would be opening gifts and Jami really wouldn't feel a part of that tradition. However, they did take gifts for her parents and siblings.

The grandparents, cousins, and other family members were very loud. Jami hadn't realized how quiet his life had become as his vision was diminishing. He realized that he was almost becoming a recluse but with Nikki in his life, that was changing.

On New Year's Eve, Jami and Nikki had a party. Jami was responsible for the balloons and party hats. Nikki took care of the rest of the decorations. Hannibal didn't like it, but he was to get a date and enjoy himself. The party was to be catered, Nikki was adamant.

The guests were due to arrive about nine o'clock, so before anyone got there, Jami and Nikki needed to talk to Hannibal.

The three of them went upstairs to Nikki's office.

"Hannibal," Jami said, "We've been so busy today that we almost forgot. We wanted to give you something special. You've always been here for me. And I've given you presents in the past, but this is something we think you'll really like."

"What do you mean? You gave me a gift already. Why are you giving me something else?"

"Well, Nikki and I thought about how much you love to cook. And you've fussed about wanting to be better at making cakes and pastries. So, this is for you." Jami handed him an envelope. Nikki was standing next to her husband grinning with anticipation.

Hannibal stared at the envelope, then frowned. "What is this?"

"Open it, open it!" Nikki struggled to remain calm.

Hannibal slowly opened the envelope. Inside were airline tickets to Paris, France, and a booklet welcoming students to a cooking school. It was all there for Hannibal. He stared in disbelief before looking up at Jami and Nikki.

"Jami, I can't go to France. I'd look like an idiot. I'm not educated like those people at that school. No! No, I'm not qualified."

"Sorry, you have to go. I've got it all arranged. I'll help you get your passport, and you won't need a visa, since the school is less than ninety days long. You'll do fine. Nikki and I have already talked to the owners of this school. We've explained that it's necessary for you to do this course because you're employed by a man with a disability and that your employer loves cake and wants you to be the best cake chef," Jami said before he started laughing.

Nikki chimed in, "Hannibal, we both love you very much. We know this is your dream. And Jami did call the school explaining that we wanted to give this as a gift to a great cook. We got you an apartment that's not far from the school, and you won't be going until next spring. You'll have time to brush up on some French phrases. And you can't say *no* because it's all paid for."

Hannibal was taken aback. Yes, this was a dream but not overseas. He just thought he'd attend a school in the Chicago area. This was too much.

Nikki had never seen Hannibal with tears in his eyes. She began to tear up as well. Jami instinctively knew Hannibal's feelings, so he stepped forward to embrace his faithful friend. Giving each other pats on the back,

Jami said, "For what you've done for me over all these years, this is something you deserve."

"Thanks, man," was all Hannibal was able to choke out before turning away.

Both Nikki and Jami knew he was deeply touched by this gesture of kindness and respect.

Guests began arriving about nine o'clock for Nikki and Jami's first party. The invitations read "attire: whatever you wanted to wear but just wear something. The only requirement was that the torso had to be covered. Nikki feared that some may come with an adult diaper and a sash.

All of Jami's law partners, spouses, and support staff came. Many hadn't seen Jami's house and were curious. Jami's sister showed up with a date. She was still fairly cool toward Nikki but since their parents were supportive of the marriage, she was gradually giving in.

Many from Nikki's office came but most didn't stay until midnight. They were curious to see where Nikki lived. They had heard how magnificent the dwelling was.

Family and friends were there. Two couples, Dave and Leigh and Phillipa and Jonathan were spending the night. They had plans for sleeping in late and watching football and eating junk food on New Year's Day.

The biggest surprise was when Jami's parents showed up. "We couldn't miss this event," James Bledsoe said. Jami was so happy to have his family in attendance. He talked to his parents for a long time and he promised to visit them in the coming week.

Jami was a great host. At home in familiar surroundings, he navigated with ease. But Nikki was always on the alert and so was Dave.

The guests were only allowed up to the second level which was more than enough area for everyone to have a wonderful experience. The caterers stayed busy making sure no one held an empty glass. The food was outstanding, with shrimp, scallops, smoked salmon, cucumber sandwiches, vegetable kabobs, and small cupcakes of chocolate and lemon flavors.

By midnight, many of the guests were close to being drunk. Nikki made sure that one member of each couple would be the designated driver. Jami found her in the crowd of guests because Nikki had made it easy for him. She had purposely worn a bright red top with gray and white striped pants.

"Have I told you how gorgeous you *look* tonight?" Jami whispered into her ear as he pulled her close.

"Yes, but I enjoy hearing you say it again."

Just then the television announced midnight, and their kiss was sweet and deep. Nikki felt dizzy from the magnitude of his love. It was as if no one else was in the room, just the two of them until they heard Dave say, "You guys need to get a room."

Slightly embarrassed, Nikki and Jami separated but still held each other around the waist.

Everyone applauded.

By two in the morning, all was quiet. Their guests had left, and the ones staying over had gone to their respective rooms.

"This was nice," Nikki said as she cuddled next to her husband.

"Yes, and I did an exceptional job at being a good host, wouldn't you say?"

"Oh, yes, most excellent."

They made love before drifting off into a sound sleep. Their life was almost perfect.

CHAPTER 6

The Second Honeymoon

Hannibal gritted his teeth for the fifth time. Jami and Nikki were driving him crazy. They were to be at O'Hare Airport by 6 a.m. and yet they were still packing. They were flying to Denver, Colorado and from there Nikki was driving a rental to their final destination. Her family had a cabin in the mountains that was near the small community of Coopersville. She and her family used to go there a couple of times a year to ski or hike. When they weren't using the cabin, they rented it out.

Nikki and Jami planned to stay two weeks and Nikki wanted Hannibal to join them during the last week. Then they would all return to Chicago by car. Nikki thought Hannibal needed to see the mountains. He'd never been West before and she felt that everyone needed to experience the Rockies.

So the plans were set. Hannibal would drive out at the beginning of the second week. Nikki, Jami, and Max would fly and have a week of skiing. Hannibal told Nikki he wouldn't ski, but that he'd like to hike and watch Jami handle the slopes.

When they had their luggage by the back door, they paused to eat. Hannibal had prepared spaghetti with meat sauce and garlic bread plus a salad and red wine. Their conversation was lively. Nikki, with excitement in her voice, explained how much Jami would enjoy skiing. His instructor would teach him all he needed to know.

"To be honest, I'm excited about doing this but still very apprehensive," Jami said.

"I think you'll do great. You're so athletic. Remember the article about the blind man who climbed Mt. Everest."

"Yes, and I'm amazed at that."

"So if he can climb Everest, you're going to do very well skiing," Nikki said.

After their meal, Jami prepared to walk Max. Nikki decided to make sure she'd packed all she wanted and needed. She also wanted to check Jami's packing.

"You go ahead and walk Max. I just want to be sure we've got everything," she said.

It was dark and cold outside. Jami and Max took their usual route. There was about an inch of snow covering the ground and the temperature was below freezing. Few people were on the street which made Jami happy. He had his cane and Max but his thoughts were on this upcoming trip.

He smiled, thinking of how he'd hesitated about dating Nikki. Dave had been right. She was just what he needed. Jami was jarred back to the present when Max yelped and began limping. "What is it boy?" he asked. Then he realized there was glass underfoot. Jami stooped down, reaching for Max's front leg. He found the injured paw and felt a piece of glass protruding from the dog's foot. He feared if he pulled it out would it bleed, but he couldn't carry Max home.

He reached into his pocket, pulled out his cell phone, and called Nikki. When she answered, he blurted out, "Get Hannibal! Max is hurt his paw has glass in it, and I can't get him home."

"Where are you?" Nikki asked.

"Our usual route, and I'm only about three blocks from the house. Some idiot must have broken a bottle. There's glass everywhere."

BLIND LOVE 001

Nikki quickly got Hannibal as she grabbed some towels and blankets. She had no idea how much blood was involved. Once they were in the car with Hannibal driving, Nikki phoned the vet.

As she spoke to the doctor, she was watching for Jami. Cars parked along the street made it difficult to see where Jami might be. Then she saw a couple of men standing by someone.

"Slow down, Hannibal. I think Jami's there where those men are." Nikki pointed in the direction on the right side of the street.

Hannibal stopped the car and hit the emergency flashers before exiting the vehicle. He ran to the men and saw Jami stooped over his pet.

"Jami, we're here. Let me pick him up for you," Hannibal said as he moved in closer in order to position himself over Max.

"Where's the car?" Jami asked as he stood upright.

One of the men offered to help as he picked up Jami's cane that he'd dropped when he tried to help Max.

"Thanks," Jami said as the stranger helped him to his car.

Hannibal suggested that Jami get in the backseat on the driver's side and he would put Max into the car from the passenger side. Nikki had already spread the blanket on the backseat. Jami sat down and Hannibal put Max into the car so that his head could rest on Jami's lap.

The blood dripping from Max's paw was slow and steady. Nikki reached over from the front seat and wrapped Max's paw in a towel. All the while, Jami spoke softly to Max as he stroked his head. Hannibal thanked the men for their help and suggested they contact the homeowner where the glass was broken. They agreed and said they'd take care of the broken glass.

Hannibal carefully merged into the traffic. Nikki told him the veterinarian would meet them at his clinic.

"Dr. Wilson said to go in the back way," Nikki informed Hannibal.

Driving down the alley to go to the back of the pet clinic, they saw the doctor's vehicle. He had just unlocked the gate protecting the rear of his facility. Dr. Wilson waved for Hannibal to drive into the open area behind the clinic. Then the doctor moved his own vehicle into the enclosure before he closed and locked the gate.

"Wait here, I've got to turn off the alarm," Dr. Wilson said as he headed toward the back door. Within minutes he told them to bring Max inside. Jami lifted Max from the backseat and carried him as Hannibal directed him into the building. Nikki brought up the rear.

The doctor suggested that Nikki wait in his office while he examined Max's foot. Both Jami and Hannibal stayed with Max as the doctor began his examination.

Two hours later all was done. The large shard of glass had gone in deep, but the doctor was able to remove the glass, clean the wound and sew everything together. With an antibiotic shot and additional medication, Max was ready to go.

"Can he travel?" Jami asked.

"No, not for a few days. I want him off of that foot as much as possible. When you say travel do you mean like a road trip?" the doctor asked.

"No, Doc, we are supposed to be getting on an airplane tomorrow morning," Nikki said as she exited the doctor's office. She didn't like to see blood or needles. She looked at Max, who was sleeping, and she walked over to pet him. Jami had not left the dog's side and Hannibal had acted as an assistant to the doctor and was leaning with his back against the cabinets.

"I'd rather Max stayed home for a couple of days. I can kennel him here if you wish."

No one said anything for a moment. Then Hannibal piped up. "I've got it. Since I wasn't going to be with you until the end of the week, I'll take care of Max and you two can go. When I join you, Max will be better, and I can bring him with me. What do you say?"

All eyes looked at Jami who had been blaming himself for Max's injury. Jami inhaled deeply, and said, "I guess that makes sense. Okay, we'll go but promise me, Hannibal, that you'll phone me daily to let us know how he's doing."

By the time they got home from the veterinary clinic and moved Max's bed downstairs, it was nearly midnight. Jami, as usual, was up before his alarm sounded. He showered and dressed before waking Nikki up with a good morning kiss. Then he made his way downstairs to check on Max. They had gotten his training crate out of the garage last night to be sure he wouldn't try to go upstairs.

As soon as Jami opened the crate door, Max tried to stand, ready to go to work with Jami. Jami sat down on the floor to reassure his faithful companion and keep him still. Max laid down and listened as if he understood exactly every word Jami was saying. Jami kept petting Max and the dog licked Jami's hand.

Hannibal appeared from the basement and asked Jami if he wanted anything to eat. They still had thirty minutes before leaving for the airport. Jami declined but said he'd go upstairs and see if Nikki wanted anything.

Nikki was pulling her sweater over her head when Jami came into their room.

"Hey, beautiful," he said.

"Morning, babe. How's Max?"

"Good. We talked—that is, I talked, he listened. I think he understood what I said. He licked my hand, but I think he was really looking forward to skiing." Jami smiled.

"I'll just bet he was." Nikki laughed at the idea of seeing Max on skis.

Getting to the airport was no problem, traffic was light. As soon as they sat down in the first-class seats and buckled in, they both fell fast asleep. They didn't wake up until the plane landed. Jami carried a backpack and had his cane. Nikki had a small backpack with their papers, and personal information and she had a rolling, carry-on bag. After collecting their luggage, they got a cart to put everything on, and Jami kept his hand on the cart handle as they made their way to the car rental area.

Once out of the airport and heading to their destination, Jami decided he was hungry. Nikki found a nice family-style restaurant not far from the highway. She put the handicap placard on the rearview mirror.

"Nikki, am I being too much trouble? You realize this is the first time we've traveled. You've got to drive, check out the car, and well, I'm just here."

They were sitting in a booth and the waitress had just brought them hot tea and a menu.

"When you asked me to marry you, I had already taken into account the fact that I'd have to do more things to be with you. I like driving, and I love being with you. So, you're no trouble because when you truly love someone, it isn't trouble, it's a joy. So please don't ever ask me something like that again. Now let me read this menu to you."

Back on the road for another two more hours, they were in the mountains. Nikki described all that she saw to give Jami an idea of the majesty of their surroundings. When they arrived at Coopersville, Nikki stopped first at the real estate office to get the keys to the cabin. Her parents owned the cabin and the two acres that surrounded it.

As Nikki was leaving the office, she almost bumped into the sheriff. "Hey, young lady," the sheriff said.

Nikki looked up at the tall, tan-faced man. "My goodness, Sheriff Bronson. It's good to see you," Nikki said as they exchanged friendly hugs. The sheriff had known Nikki and her family for ten years. Nikki's father and the sheriff had an unbreakable bond over time.

"So, you're here?"

"Yes, my husband and I are here to ski. Come over to the car and meet him."

After introductions were made, the sheriff shared that Mr. Townsend had called him sometime in the past week. He wanted to tell him that his daughter and her husband were coming to ski. "So I'm glad I saw you. Now that I know you're here you'll have to come to dinner at my house. My wife makes a great chili and I make great cornbread."

"Thanks, we'd like that," Jami said. He liked the friendliness of the sheriff's voice.

After the sheriff's departure, they needed to make one more stop. They had to go to the ski rental shop. They needed to rent skis for downhill skiing, as well as for cross-country skiing, plus poles, boots, and footwear for the cross-country skis. Once they were fitted the sales associate put the skis and poles on the roof rack of the red rental jeep. Nikki had Jami put their rental equipment into the backseat of the vehicle while she paid. The young man helped Jami with the boots, although Jami was good about his surroundings.

After driving out of town onto the state roadway, they drove to the cabin just three miles away. The driveway was plowed, and the front porch was swept clean of snow and ice. Before they got out of the car, Nikki told Jami how many steps were up to the porch, and that the door was directly in front of the steps.

Nikki went up first to unlock the door, then she called Jami to come ahead. Jami first went to the back of the jeep and got the large luggage bag, and his backpack. Then he carefully walked toward the front stairs. After one foot touched the bottom stair, he walked up and into the cabin.

BLIND LOVE 001

It was a two-story structure, so Nikki guided Jami up the stairway to the second floor.

"Are you okay?" Nikki asked.

"Yes, it's just new, I've got to get my bearings, but I like the quiet. So, let's get everything unloaded."

They did just that. Nikki explained there was a box to the left of the front door that was about hip height, and he could place the skis and poles there. She asked that he only put the cross-country skis there because the next day they were skiing downhill.

While Jami was busy figuring out which skis needed to stay on the jeep and which ones to place on the porch, Nikki got out the rest of their luggage. She also checked to make sure the refrigerator and the pantry were stocked with the food she'd requested.

When she returned to the doorway to see how Jami was doing, he was sitting on the step just staring out.

He'd placed the skis where they belonged and now was enjoying the beauty that was around them. The sky was blue with white puffy clouds floating by. The wind caused a whistling throughout the pines behind the cabin. Nikki sat down next to him, looping her arm through his.

"This is nice," he said. "I didn't realize how stressed I'd been feeling but now I'm good. Thanks, Babe." Then he kissed her on the top of her head.

"You're welcome," Nikki said as she rested her head on his shoulder. "How much can you see?"

"I can make out the movement of the Aspen trees and when I tilt my head I can appreciate the beautiful blue sky. The snow is so white. Yes, this will be a trip I'll remember."

The next morning, they were up and ready for skiing. Nikki fixed pancakes, sausage, sliced apples, and hot tea for breakfast. She packed protein bars and water in their backpacks for if they got hungry. Driving to the ski resort, Nikki told Jami that he'd be with an instructor who was trained to teach individuals with limited vision. And that he would be wearing a vest that says in large letters *blind skier*.

"So where will you be?" Jami asked.

"I'll be with you, but I'm not going to talk much. You'll need to focus on what your instructor says. I think you'll begin on a beginners' slope and then he'll take you up to other slopes. You're gonna have so much fun!"

Nikki said. "And I'm videoing all of it. I'm sure our families will love to see you conquering the mountains on skis."

When they arrived at the base lodge there were already several skiers present. Nikki found a spot close to the lodge. They put on their ski boots before getting out of their vehicle. Then Jami got out of the jeep and began unhooking the skis and poles from the roof of their car. With Nikki's help, he put his skis and the poles on one shoulder. After Nikki got her skis and poles on her own shoulder, she had Jami put his hand on her free shoulder as they carefully walked toward a large building that housed a restaurant, bar, restrooms, and where they would check in for ski lessons.

Nikki had emailed ahead, and she'd gotten the name of Jami's instructor. So, after leaning their skis against a railing outside, they went in. Jami kept hold of Nikki's shoulder, but all of his senses were on high alert. He could see a lot of people moving in bright colorful clothing. His sense of smell picked up the aroma of coffee and breakfast foods being cooked. All of the voices he heard were people who sounded happy and excited about being there.

When they got to a desk, Nikki spoke to a young woman about lessons for Jami and she told her that Todd Larsen was to be his instructor. The woman looked through some papers and found their information. She gave Nikki their lift passes and Jami a vest that identified him as a blind skier. Then the woman directed Nikki where outside to meet Todd, saying he'd be there in about five minutes.

"Are you alright?" Nikki asked Jami as they trooped outside.

"I'm fine, just a little nervous. I've never skied, and you know skiing isn't a black man's sport."

"Really, now. Well, please don't tell that to my dad or brothers," Nikki joked.

"Nikki, you know what I mean, so don't give me grief. I'm looking forward to this experience."

Before Nikki could reply a handsome, blue-eyed young man approached. He was a little shorter than Jami so he must have been just six feet tall. He was wearing a tee shirt with ski pants held up with suspenders.

"Hi, I'm Todd, and you must be Jami and Nikki. I've been looking forward to meeting you both. Hope you don't mind me calling you by your first names."

"Nope, we're okay with that," Jami said.

"Okay, so Nikki, you are an intermediate skier, right? And Jami, you've never skied, is that correct?"

They nodded. So Todd began explaining where they would go and how he'd be with Jami all day. They would take a lunch break and then hit the slopes again in the afternoon for a couple more hours. "Then you'll be tired and just want to go home and sleep."

Nikki was more nervous than Jami, but Todd was so patient with her husband. Todd even suggested that Nikki go skiing and then come back in an hour. Nikki took his advice. After kissing Jami, she got her skis and poles and got in line for one of the chair lifts.

Todd explained everything Jami needed to know. How to relax his knees, how to move his feet when he needed to stop or slow down. Todd also told Jami that he would be in front, holding on to Jami's ski poles, while guiding him down the hill. They worked for a while so that Jami could become accustomed to the feel of the skis and ski boots. Todd also explained how to walk with the skis on and how to turn around. Then they went to the easy slopes. With Jami in tow, they glided down the hill. It was a meandering, wide ski run.

Jami could hear the voices of people who passed him and called out encouraging words. Jami focused on Todd's voice. He could tell from that voice that Todd was young. Jami guessed that his instructor was in his early twenties.

As the day progressed, Jami became confident on his skis. He'd progressed from the rope tow to the chair lift. By now, Nikki was with them. Although Todd continued to guide Jami, Nikki stayed close. She was proud of her husband and he looked good even when he fell a couple of times.

During lunch, Jami excitedly talked about skiing and said he enjoyed it more than he'd thought. He said even falling wasn't bad, although getting the skis straight and going in the correct direction was a challenge. He laughed at himself and for Nikki that was nice because, at times, Jami couldn't see the humor in his mistakes.

By two in the afternoon, they were spent. After loading their equipment onto the ski rack on the roof of their vehicle, Nikki drove to town. She wanted to walk around a bit without the heavy ski boots on. They stopped at a little coffee house and got tea and scones. They'd decided when they returned to the cabin, they'd take a much-needed nap before dinner.

The fresh air was invigorating, but the air was also thin, and physical activities were really tiring. The week went by quickly. Their schedule was downhill skiing one day and cross-country skiing the next. Jami decided that he was getting in better physical shape from all that they were doing. Every evening they enjoyed being together. Sometimes they'd read or listen to music and dance. But they always made love each night before falling asleep.

Sunday morning, Nikki and Jami awoke late. They had not stopped skiing for the entire week. They were tired and Sunday was to be a day off. Jami had spoken to Hannibal the night before. Max was well on the road to walking normally and they'd be leaving Chicago Sunday morning so they should arrive in Colorado that evening.

As they cuddled together in bed, Nikki suggested they just stay around the house. Jami agreed before nibbling her ear. "This has been one of the best vacations I've ever had," he whispered softly.

Nikki changed positions to look at Jami's face. She'd become accustomed to looking into his eyes. His eyes were hazel, and it was still difficult for her to believe he couldn't see clearly. He had long lashes, the kind that women desire, and his skin was brown and flawless. But it was his smile and the tone of his voice that caused her heart to beat faster.

"You're looking at me again," he said with a smile.

"You have beautiful eyes."

"That's what all my wives have said," he teased before kissing her lips.

Nikki couldn't imagine what her life would be without Jami. He was the man she needed, and she knew that he felt the same way about her. It was hard to believe that just a year ago she'd seen him at the banquet where she'd modeled the dress for Connie. Now, Connie had a thriving clothing design business, thanks to Merl Swinson. Dave and Leigh were buying her former dwelling, and Phillipa and Jonathan were planning on getting married this summer. Life in just twelve months had changed for all of them, but the changes were wonderful.

Reluctantly, Nikki got out of the bed. She wanted to cook breakfast, make bread and bake a cake for Hannibal today. She removed her rings because she'd be working with dough and hated to get her rings dirty. Jami had fallen back asleep but as soon as he heard her in the shower, he woke up.

BLIND LOVE 001

After her warm shower, she dressed in a long-sleeve tee shirt, and over that a bulky sweater. She pulled on fleece-lined tights over her lace panties, then tugged on some thick socks. They kept the cabin cool, about sixty degrees. By the time she finished dressing, Jami was in the shower.

As Nikki made her way downstairs, she felt a cold draft. Rolling her eyes and shaking her head, she knew that the back door must have opened. They'd complained to the agent to get it fixed but it hadn't happened yet.

Going to give her a piece of my mind, Nikki thought, going toward the kitchen.

As she went through the swinging door, she froze when a male voice behind her said, "Stop lady, don't move." Nikki did as she was told. She was scared, then more so when she saw another man come from the pantry. He had a gun in his hand.

"Who else is here with you?" the man in front of her asked.

"My husband."

"OK, good. You come over here and stand by me," he told her as he motioned with the pistol to move toward him.

Nikki's feet felt like lead but she somehow managed to walk. This man was average height with dirty blonde hair. He had a teardrop tattoo by one eye and other tattoos on his neck and the back of his hand. As soon as she was close, he reached out grabbing her arm, pulling her closer to him. He then poked the gun into her ribs so hard that she winced.

The intruder nuzzled his face into Nikki's hair, which was a riot of curls framing her face. Then he moved down to her neck. "You smell good," he muttered. "It's been a while since I've been with a woman."

Before Nikki could respond, they heard Jami descending the stairs. The taller man who was stationed behind the door motioned for quiet. When Jami pushed open the door, she and the man holding her were in Jami's line of sight.

As soon as Jami stepped into the kitchen, he made out two forms. "Who…?" That was the only word that came out of his mouth before he felt an extremely sharp pain on the back of his head.

Nikki screamed Jami's name as she watched in horror as her beloved fell to the kitchen floor. Blood oozed from the back of his head. Nikki struggled to go to him, but the man had her in a firm grip.

"But I have to see if he's alright," she pleaded.

"He ain't dead," said the man who'd hit Jami.

"Oh, please can I just make sure?"

Then the man who'd struck Jami aimed his gun near Jami's head—then pulled the trigger. The shot was deafening inside the house, the bullet leaving a smoking hole in the floor only inches from Jami's head.

"If you say one more time that you need to check your husband, I'll make sure that he's dead. Understand?" He grinned, showing yellow teeth and gums that were evidence of drug abuse.

Nikki could only nod. Her heart was hurting and her stomach was in knots. She felt weak, angry, and helpless.

"Now fix us something to eat," the man holding Nikki said. "Then we'll get out of here."

As Nikki prepared a meal for the men, she kept trying to figure out a way to gain her and Jami's freedom. While she cooked, one of the men went upstairs. She had already told them that they had very little cash because they used debit or credit cards. They took the small amount of cash they found. They also took one of Jami's credit cards.

After they finished eating, they had Nikki get her coat and boots. They were taking her with them. Jami had not stirred although his head had stopped bleeding.

After dragging Nikki from the house, they put her into the passenger seat. The taller man named Chuck drove, and the man who had held Nikki got into the back. She'd heard Chuck call that man Sam. Nikki could feel tears forming in her eyes and rolling down her cheeks as she watched their honeymoon lodge recede. She'd been able to suppress crying earlier but now she couldn't stop.

"Stop your sniffling," Chuck growled. "We ain't gonna hurt you. You're just insurance until we can put some distance between us and the state police."

"You said I could have her before we let her go. You promised me," Sam whined from the backseat. "I've never been with a pretty woman before."

"First we gotta get out of this state."

BLIND LOVE 001

Jami slowly began to regain consciousness. His head was pounding. He attempted to stand, then felt dizzy so he stopped moving for a moment while on his hands and knees. His mind was in a fog. Something had hit him hard on the back of his head. Then like a tsunami everything came rushing into his mind. He recalled Nikki with a man standing beside her. She screamed his name, then all went dark.

"*Nikki!*"

Jami forced himself to stand, reaching out and finding a chair for help. Calling his wife's name he stumbled around the kitchen at first, then he made his way through the rest of the house. He worried that whoever knocked him out might have tied her up somewhere in the house.

After a thorough search, Jami found their cell phones and tablets, but they were all smashed. He had to find help. After yanking on his boots and a down jacket, he went outside. In his pain and confusion, his sense of direction was off. As he walked through the snow drifts trying to find a roadway, he suddenly realized that he was going in the opposite direction. He had been heading for the area that Nikki had warned him about.

He remembered, "*Jami, when Dad bought this house, he loved the view from the cliff on the back side of the property just beyond the pine trees. So please don't go there alone.*"

In his confused state of mind, he had been heading in that direction. His only thoughts were still of his beloved wife. He had to find her. He had to get help to locate her.

"*Nikki!,*" Jami called out again and he started to turn around. But that was his last thought before he stepped out into thin air.

CHAPTER 7

Where's Jami?

Hannibal drove leisurely through the town of Coopersville. He liked what he saw. It was a ski town nestled among the mountains of Colorado. There were many shops selling winter clothing, skis, and ski accessories, and many were having sales because the season was ending. Shop owners needed to make the switch from winter to summer clothing and souvenirs.

His drive from Chicago had been easy, and he'd stayed overnight because there was no hurry. He'd spoken to Jami the night before and all was well. So he figured that he and Max would take their time and arrive early Monday morning. Nikki had given him specific directions on how to locate the cabin. As he approached the house, something didn't seem right. He didn't see their vehicle parked out front, and when he stopped his car, he noticed the front door was ajar.

Hannibal's instincts went into high alert. He told Max to stay as he slowly got out of the car. There was a light dusting of snow on the steps and the porch. He carefully pushed open the front door. When he stepped into the hallway, all was quiet. *Too quiet.* He didn't like it.

He called out Nikki and Jami's names and got no answer, so he began walking around the house. He went through the living room and into the kitchen. There were dirty dishes everywhere. Then he noticed the blood on the floor. The back door was open. His heart sank. Could something have happened to Nikki or Jami? Did they have an emergency and had to rush to town?

He left the kitchen and went upstairs. There he found clothing tossed everywhere. He also noticed their cell phones and their computers were crushed as if someone had stomped on them with a heavy shoe or boot. He stepped over the clothing lying on the floor and went into the bathroom. Whenever Nikki was going to bake, she removed her rings and put them in a special place. "I don't want to get dough on them," she had told him once when they were home, and he was teaching her one of his recipes. He found her make-up bag and inside was a small silk pouch. He opened it and her rings were there. He put them in his inside jacket pocket. He didn't know why but something told him he should.

Hannibal hurried from the house. He needed to find the police or sheriff or whatever law enforcement was available in town.

Upon returning to Coopersville, he saw signs pointing to the hospital, city hall, and the sheriff's office. When he got there, he hurried inside. A woman deputy was typing at a computer when he approached the wooden desk.

She slowly looked up at him. Hannibal couldn't read her facial expression. He knew that being an African-American at a ski resort was rare but he needed help.

"May I help you, sir?" Her voice was impersonal.

"Yes, my name is Hannibal Jackson and I need to speak to the sheriff."

"Has there been an accident of some sort?" she asked, her voice cool as her eyes locked in on Hannibal's face and build.

"I don't know. I'm here to meet my employer and his wife. They were staying in a cabin about two or three miles from town."

As he was speaking, the sheriff strolled in from a back room situated behind the front desk. "Are you Hannibal?" he asked.

"Yes, how did you know?"

"I'm Sheriff Bronson. Nikki told me you were expected this weekend. Didn't you find their place?'

"That's just it. Sheriff, they are not there. There's blood on the kitchen floor and the place has been ransacked," the words tumbling out of Hannibal like an avalanche. "I didn't know if Jami had gotten hurt and

Nikki had to rush him to the hospital. I found their cell phones and computers damaged."

"Did you touch anything?" the sheriff asked as he was in the process of putting on his jacket and hat.

Hannibal shook his head.

The sheriff turned to the woman and told her to check the hospital to find out if a Mr. Jamison Bledsoe had been admitted. Then he told her to get a deputy to meet him out at the cabin. He explained the location to her.

"Hannibal, can I call you Hannibal?"

Hannibal nodded.

"Okay, you follow me."

Driving at a high rate of speed, the sheriff in his SUV, Hannibal stayed close behind him in the Benz. The roads weren't too slippery, mostly just wet as the snow melt was beginning and water covered the roadway

When they reached the cabin, the sheriff had Hannibal stay in the Benz. He wanted to check the place out. Within minutes, he reappeared at the front door to wave Hannibal inside. At the same time, another patrol vehicle pulled in behind the sheriff's SUV.

Hannibal had rolled down the windows to the car before he got out so Max could get some air. All three of the men walked inside. The sheriff and his deputy checked everything. Sheriff Bronson had his deputy call for the state police.

"Hannibal, something did happen here, and it doesn't look good. I hate to say this, but we're looking for two escaped convicts. We thought they were in another part of the state but obviously, we were wrong."

"When you say *criminals*, what are you talking about?"

"One was serving time for manslaughter and the other for murder and rape."

Hannibal sighed. He didn't want to lose his temper, but this was ridiculous.

"It looks like this all must have happened sometime this morning. What time did you get here?"

"Around noon."

The sheriff began questioning Hannibal again. An hour later the yard was filled with state patrol cars and crime scene investigators were checking everywhere for fingerprints.

BLIND LOVE 001

Hannibal went outside to get Max. He walked the dog away from the house. They were just in the way. All Hannibal could think about was how would he tell Jami and Nikki's parents that their children were missing? Who would he phone first? What could he say? His stomach ached from the anxiety.

As he and Max turned around to go back to the cabin, Max began acting excited. When they got closer to the cabin, Max stuck his nose into the snow and then whimpered. It was the whimper he used when he was trying to locate Jami.

A few weeks after Jami and Nikki were married, they'd come up with a game. It was hide and seek for Max. They took turns. One would take Max outside in the backyard while the other one would hide somewhere in the house. Then Max had to locate the one hiding. Of course, Max would be rewarded when he found whoever the subject was. But the interesting thing was that Max had developed a particular whimper for Jami and a different one for Nikki.

This time it was Jami's whimper. Max pulled Hannibal away from the dwelling, and toward the trees. Hannibal had to forcefully stop Max. *Could the dog know something?*

Hannibal called one of the state troopers to have Sheriff Bronson come outside. It took a few minutes but soon the sheriff was standing next to Hannibal. Then he explained to Sheriff Bronson how the dog was acting and why. "Would it be alright if I let Max take me where the scent is leading him?" Hannibal asked.

"I'll go with you if you don't mind. Those state guys don't need a small-town sheriff like me hanging around. Let's go."

At first, Max seemed to know exactly which direction he needed to go. He paused, then stuck his snout back into the snow, almost covering his eyes. Suddenly, he took off bounding over the white powder. Hannibal and the sheriff followed, trying to keep up with the canine.

The sun was getting low, and the tall Pine and Aspen shadows made it seem even later in the day than it was. The sheriff produced a flashlight from his utility belt as they forged ahead.

"We'd better slow down," Sheriff Bronson said. "If I remember correctly, there's a ledge near here. It's a long drop."

Hannibal pulled Max's leash in closer but not too much because he could see that the dog was anxious to receive his treat for finding Jami.

Suddenly, the sheriff grabbed Hannibal by the arm. The cliff appeared in front of them. They both stopped just in time. And Max almost went over the edge.

"*Wow!*" Hannibal said, as he looked out over a beautiful valley. In the meantime, Max had dropped down to his stomach and was whimpering again.

All was silent, except Max. Then Hannibal heard it. He commanded Max, "Quiet." Then he heard it again.

"Sheriff, listen." Both men strained their ears.

"*Help, help me.*" It was barely audible. The voice low and hoarse was coming from below the ledge.

Both men flopped onto their stomachs to look over the cliffside. Sheriff Bronson shined his flashlight down in the direction of the voice. It took a few seconds, but they finally saw a figure laying on an outcropping of rocks. It was Jami.

"*Jami!*" Hannibal shouted. "Oh, my god!" He choked back tears.

"Jami, this is Rusty—Sheriff Bronson. Your friend Hannibal is here, too. Don't you dare move. I'll call for help."

What seemed like an eternity took only a little more than an hour. The first responders showed up in the ambulance. One of the EMTs happened to be Jami's ski instructor, Todd.

They secured one end of their ropes to the rescue vehicle's winch on the front of the ambulance. Then two of the first responders rappelled fifty feet down the side of the cliff to where Jami lay. They examined him and found he'd broken his leg, and possibly his collar bone. They radioed the sheriff to have the backboard lowered so that they could strap him securely onto it and lift him out safely. Before they signaled to lift him, they also placed a brace around his neck. They worked amazingly fast for being tethered to ropes.

Once Jami was secured the sheriff, Hannibal, and several deputies slowly pulled Jami up. The winch on the ambulance also pulled the two EMTs up the cliff. It was a tedious process but finally Jami was safe. Quickly they carried him to the ambulance. Max stayed right by Jami's side. At the ambulance, Max tried to get in, but they wouldn't let him.

"Hannibal, did you find Nikki?" Jami's voice croaked as he spoke.

"Not yet," Hannibal said.

Before closing the back door of the ambulance Todd told Hannibal to meet at the hospital.

Hannibal paced in the hospital waiting room, but he wasn't alone. Sheriff Rusty Bronson walked the floor too. Both men were lost in their own thoughts. Jami was being examined and having his leg set. The doctors were also checking for any other injuries he may have suffered from his fall. Max lay on the floor by the chairs, but he seemed anxious as if he knew that his master was hurt, and he needed to be with him.

Finally, a doctor appeared and explained that because of Jami's excellent health and good physical condition he had no internal injuries. The leg would heal quickly, and his collarbone was bruised but not broken. He had a deep head wound that they were able to stitch up, but the doctor felt that it would heal without leaving much of a scar. He had suffered some frostbite on his cheeks and nose but fortunately gloves and good boots kept his appendages frostbite free. They wanted to keep him overnight for observation. He would be able to leave the hospital the next day.

"Can we talk to him?" Sheriff Bronson asked.

"I'd rather you wait until morning. His throat is raw from yelling in the cold air. I've given him a sedative." the doctor said.

After thanking the doctor, Hannibal heaved a sigh of relief.

"Hannibal, if you don't mind, I'll phone Nikki's family. I know them. You call Jami's folks. It's a hard call to make but I've had more practice than you," Rusty said.

"Thanks, sheriff but what will you say about Nikki?"

"I'll explain to Tom that Nikki is missing. I'm sure we'll find her alive. Then I'll tell them about Jami and his situation. I can only tell them what I know. We're going to continue looking for her and I won't give up. She is a lovely woman and this is a rescue."

"Sheriff, do you mind waiting until morning before calling Nikki's family? I'd like to check on Jami and see how he's doing."

"You know what, that's a better idea. Then I'll have the chance to hear from Jami what happened. I'll bring one of the state boys with me."

Hannibal asked the sheriff for the nearest motel so he could rest and take care of the dog. He didn't want to be too far away from the hospital, but he was so weary he couldn't think straight. He hadn't eaten anything all day, and poor Max was confused. Rusty directed him to a nice place only a block from the hospital. Rusty told him that he'd give them a call to expect him and the dog, and he'd tell them that they were his special friends. He also mentioned that there was a diner that was open late if he wanted to get something to eat.

By midnight Hannibal and Max were asleep.

Hannibal awoke at about six the next morning. His body felt stiff and his head hurt. Max was still sleeping. Hannibal went to shower and get into some clean clothes. While walking Max, Hannibal remembered how he and Jami had a few close calls with disgruntled clients. Once a client's husband tried to attack Jami because he felt that his wife shouldn't have gotten a prison sentence. Hannibal recalled the irate husband's voice, "I love her! How will I live without her? You wait—someday you'll lose the person you love the most. Then you'll know how I feel!" He then lunged at Jami with a knife ready to stab him. Hannibal had blocked that attempt. The wife was a three-time loser, so Jami couldn't get her a reduced sentence.

Hannibal also recalled how Jami had helped him change his life for the better. He had been in foster care most of his life. His grandmother finally took him in and she did the best she could, but Hannibal was angry and in trouble often. If Jami hadn't been his public defender and seen something in him, Hannibal was sure he'd be dead or in jail with a long-term sentence. Now Jami needed his help, and he was determined to do all he could no matter what.

Hannibal had gotten permission to go back to the cabin to retrieve Jami and Nikki's clothes and toiletries. There was still yellow police tape across the door, but the sheriff had said it was alright for him to enter and get the clothes. It was so quiet except for the wind gracefully moving the few leaves of the Aspen trees. It was hard for him to imagine this lovely place as a scene of horror. He quickly gathered everything and left. Much of the snow was melting and green grass was beginning to make an appearance.

BLIND LOVE 001

After unloading the car, he headed for the hospital leaving Max alone. The doctor had said Jami would be released, and he needed to bring clothes for him to wear.

※

By nine-thirty, he was asking the nurse where Jami's room was. When he got there, the sheriff and a detective were talking to Jami. He entered the room and greetings were exchanged. Jami's smile, however slight, indicated that he was better—but concern showed in his face.

Rusty nodded. "So, you look rested."

"Yes, I was whipped but I'm better," Hannibal said and turned to Jami. "How are *you* feeling?"

"I'm okay, my throat hurts. I don't know how long I called for help. I think I lost consciousness for a time after falling over that ledge. When I realized my situation, I was scared. I pressed myself as far away from the side of the cliff as I could. Then I began to yell."

"We're glad you did," the detective said. "But it was your dog who really found you, you know."

"Yes, I remember someone telling me that as I was being put into the ambulance. And was one of the men who helped me named Todd?" Jami asked.

"Why, yes," the sheriff said.

"I thought that's what he said as he was hanging on the side of that mountain. Please tell him thanks. He's a good young man—and a great ski instructor. Now Rusty, what are you doing to find Nikki?"

"Everything we can," Rusty said, but he couldn't hide the worry that was apparent on his face. "Our department and the state troopers are combing the area. We're expecting snow tonight, so we're pushing hard to find her before it hits. It is our priority."

Just then the doctor came in to let Jami know that he could leave anytime. He had checked on all of his tests and X-rays and everything looked good.

"Just take it easy for a few days. I want to see you in two weeks. You should be able to get out of the cast and into a walking boot, by then." The doctor nodded toward the men in the room before leaving.

"Two weeks...but Jami aren't you going to go home?" the sheriff asked.

"No, I can't leave without my wife. I'll stay as long as it takes."

Hannibal, the sheriff, and the detective were quiet for a long moment.

"Jami," Hannibal said. "I understand, but we can't stay at the cabin and this could take a long time."

"Like I said, as long as it takes. I won't leave the most important part of me that's missing. Nikki is my heart. Do you think I'd leave without my heart?"

"You two must understand this. Nikki is my life, my heart, and I can't leave without her. I feel—no, *I know* that she's alive. It's just going to take time and I'm willing to wait. Hannibal, you find us a place where we can lodge long-term. It has to be furnished and we'll move in there. It's near the end of March. We weren't planning to leave for another week. We'll just tack on another three. By then, I should be able to get around better. That will put us into the middle of April."

Jami had thought everything out and Hannibal knew by the tone of his voice that it was to be done as he'd said. Before leaving the room, the detective thanked Jami for talking with him again. The sheriff said he would phone his wife and that she might know of a place that would be available.

Rusty added, "Jami, I'd plan on calling Nikki's family. I think they should hear from you."

"Yes, I'll do that. I'm sure Tom will want to speak to you also."

"That's fine. He can call me anytime. I'll go now to see how the investigation is going." Rusty then reached out his hand to shake Jami's.

After the sheriff's exit, Jami told Hannibal, "I want to talk to my in-laws, now."

"I understand. I'll go get Max and walk around the town a little since we'll be here for a while."

When Hannibal walked out, Jami inhaled deeply before making the call he never imagined he'd have to make.

As soon as Jami heard Tom's voice, he tried to speak, but he seemed to lose his voice for a second. Finally, he said, "Tom, I need to tell you some very bad news. Please sit down and if MariAnn is close she needs to hear this as well." As he told his in-laws all that he could recall and what the police officials had surmised had happened, their sobs were heart-wrenching.

Jami tried to control his tears but to no avail. His emotional wounds were too raw. After that conversation, Jami needed to compose himself. He had no idea how his parents would react but he did know that they loved Nikki and would be very upset.

Jami then phoned his folks.

"Jami! We didn't expect to hear from you for another week," Leah said. "Is everything going well? How do you like skiing?"

"Mom, something has happened. Is Dad home? You both need to hear this."

"Oh…yes. I'll call him."

As Jami waited he inhaled deeply. He had purposely phoned his mother's cell phone because, if he'd phoned his father, he would have to tell the story twice.

"What is it, son?" James' deep voice boomed over the phone.

Jami knew he was on speaker and, as he spoke, he heard his mother cry out. He continued talking, afraid if he stopped he'd break down again.

When Jami finished, his father asked what they could do to help.

"I've decided to stay here until Nikki is found. I can't come home without her."

"Let's hope that will be soon—but it could even take weeks," James said.

"I'm prepared to wait. Dad, if it was Mom, wouldn't you feel the same way? If there is any possibility that she's alive I have to be here."

His mother's sobs could be heard over his father's deep, emotional breaths.

"You're right, Jami. And I know that Hannibal and Max are there. What about your cases?"

"I'll be calling Jack to explain the situation. He and Jonell can work together getting postponements. And then I'll phone Dave. He knows most of our close friends. I don't know if this will be in the Chicago papers—but it'll likely show up on at least a few of the national news' Websites. I'll contact everyone I can think of."

"That sounds like a plan. You know whatever we can do, just let us know," Jamison said.

"Thanks, Dad. I can't leave without Nikki."

Before he could end the conversation, Jami's mother said, "Jami, I want to come out to be with you. What kind of mother would I be if I sat here waiting for who knows what?"

"Mom, really!" Jami said. "I'm grown and I'm not helpless. Tell you what, wait for two weeks. Let's see what happens. We've gotta find Nikki by then."

"Oh…okay, but if not…."

"We'll talk about it then," Jami said.

After disconnecting, Jami leaned back onto his pillows and sighed deeply.

With a couple minutes to pause, reflect and rest, Jami called his law partner to apprise him of the situation.

"Don't worry about anything," Jack's voice was reassuring. "Jonell and I will take care of everything. I just want both you and Nikki to be back with us as soon as possible."

Jami agreed, "So do I. Please let everyone know what's going on."

The two friends continued talking for nearly an hour. After Jami ended the call, he considered his next task…he had to phone Dave. It would be another uncomfortable conversation.

"Hey, Jami, why are you calling me? Don't you have *better* things to do—I mean, *isn't* this your *honeymoon?*" Dave's voice was always enthusiastic.

There was no way around it. Jami had to just get to the point. "Dave, our cabin was broken into and Nikki is missing."

"What do you mean missing? When did this happen?"

"Sunday. We'd had a great week of skiing, and we were looking forward to greeting Hannibal and Max. When I entered the kitchen, I could make out a man holding Nikki. Then something hit me on the back of the head. I remember hearing Nikki scream before I blacked out."

"*My god, man!*" Dave exclaimed.

"When I came too, I was dizzy but all I wanted was Nikki—to see if she was okay. My legs were wobbly when I tried to stand. I screamed out her name—I was frantic. Finally, once I got my footing, I searched every room in the place. I figured…*hoped* that whoever had broken in had tied her up somewhere in the house. But she wasn't there."

"So, you got help?" Dave began firing questions like a lit string of firecrackers. "Are you okay, now? What are the police telling you?

"Slow down, and I'll tell you everything. Anyway, when I couldn't find Nikki in the house, I grabbed my coat and went outside hoping to find her someplace nearby. But, in my confusion, I walked in the wrong direction. I didn't realize I was going toward a cliff and not the road."

"Please don't tell me…."

"Yes, I went over. Fortunately, I slid down most of the way, and I ended up landing on an outcropping. I don't how long I was there—several hours. I was in and out of consciousness."

"How did you get rescued?"

"Max and Hannibal found me. And Hannibal got a hold of the sheriff."

"Are you in the hospital now?"

"Yeah, I stayed overnight." Jami cleared his throat. It was still raw. "Getting ready to leave now. I have a broken leg and a bruised collarbone. Otherwise, I'm doing pretty well…*physically*."

"*Sheesh*…is there anything I can do?"

"Yeah, would you please call our close friends? Let them know what happened. Oh, and you met Natasha, Nikki's broker?"

"Yes, I've got her information."

"Call her and let her know," Jami said. "But ask her to call me tomorrow. I'm talked out for today."

"Don't worry, I'll take care of that. Anything else?"

"No, I think that's all for now. Thanks, man, you're the best." Jami said. After a few more words of encouragement from Dave they hung up.

<hr />

Since the ski season was ending and many rentals were now vacated, Jami, Hannibal, and Max were soon settled into a comfortable two-bedroom house. The kitchen was furnished with cookware as well as plates, glassware, and everything a kitchen would need. Rusty's wife loaned them some additional pots and pans.

Jami stayed in constant contact with his office, and he got continuances for a number of his court cases. His sister Jonell worked hard to make sure Jami knew exactly what was going on. She found another attorney who was willing to handle one of his cases.

Nikki's office, with the help of her assistant, took care of the properties that she managed. They, too, were hopeful that she would be coming home soon.

After they moved into the rental house Jami asked Hannibal for Nikki's cosmetic bag. It was his wife's fragrance he was after. He'd learned to love the clean, soft fragrance—never overpowering but it was *her*, and he loved it. Jami had gotten into the ritual of inhaling that fragrance just before going to sleep. He was afraid that if he didn't do it every night, he might forget one of the things that made her so special.

Jami continued improving, determined to heal as quickly as possible. He had reasoned with his mother that she shouldn't come. That he and Hannibal had gotten into a good routine. And the sheriff's wife had volunteered to help whenever Hannibal needed to run errands.

"Jami," Hannibal said, "it's been a month already."

"Yes, I know. But we're doing alright. The sheriff's department is still searching for the rental car. I'm able to have Zoom meetings with my office. Most of the people here in town are getting to know us—especially Max."

"Yes, it seems Max has become very popular," Hannibal agreed. "But Jami, you haven't considered how I feel about living here."

After a pause for thought, Jami finally said, "I'm sorry, you're right. I've been too busy focusing on my own feelings. How do you feel about being here?"

"To be honest, I've been ruminating on it. I've never thought of living anywhere else except in the city. I love Chicago. Jami, you are not only my employer but my best friend. I've known you longer than anyone else in my whole life and please know that I care deeply about Nikki. She is the best thing that's happened to us.

"But please consider the repercussions of this decision, We can't stay here forever," Hannibal said, his voice calm and sincere.

"Hannibal, what will I do without her?" Jami asked, feeling an emptiness and aching in his chest. "We only had one year together."

Hannibal got up from the chair and walked over to Jami. He patted his friend's shoulder. "I understand and I know going back to Chicago will be hard. Believe me, when I think about the house with no Nikki my heart breaks also. But we need to go home. The people here are really nice, but Chicago is our home."

BLIND LOVE 001

"I know you're right," Jami said, his head bowed in resignation. "I was so sure she'd be with us by now. I hate to admit it, but you are right. Give me a couple of days to figure out what I want to do."

⁂

For the next two days, Jami carefully considered Hannibal's words. He also thought about Chicago which made him smile thinking of the fun and zany things Nikki had him do; the first bike ride and how they fell off and laughed as they got back to their feet—then there was the parachute jump. He never thought he'd do anything like that. And then, how about her having him climb a rock wall and jogging outside with Max. Yes, she had opened up the world that he thought was lost because of his blindness.

Even on this trip, skiing had been so much fun. He'd loved the nights by the fireplace talking, laughing, kissing, and being in love. But now, he was alone again, and his world had become a very lonely, dark, and cold place.

"Hannibal, tell you what. Let's stay here a couple more weeks. That will be the first part of May. If we don't know anything more by then, I'll return to Chicago. Would that be alright with you?"

CHAPTER 8

Where is Nikki?

It's too hot, Nikki thought. She felt heat coming from a source directly in front of her. But where was she? Nikki slowly opened her eyes. She faced a large stone fireplace and a blazing fire. *No wonder I'm hot*, she thought, *but where am I?*

A heavy quilt lay over her, and she realized she was only wearing a tee shirt and panties.

Closing her eyes, she tried to understand her situation. The fireplace didn't look familiar and the quilt that covered her wasn't something that she recognized.

She slowly scanned her surroundings.

Above her was a vaulted ceiling with beautiful wooden beams and a skylight partially covered with snow. There were stairs leading to a second floor.

A rustling came from behind her. She seemed to be on a couch, and someone was moving about on the other side of the sofa where she lay. *What should I do?*

The heat from the fireplace was just too much.

Nikki stirred and began moving out from under the quilt. When she moved she felt stiff and needed to stretch. She moaned, softly. Then there was a man's voice.

"So, you're finally awake."

The figure of a tall man appeared standing behind the sofa. His hair was black and edged lightly in gray, and two long braids of it lay over his broad shoulders. His tan face had weathered lines spreading out from the corners of his dark eyes as if he'd lived in the desert.

"I wondered if you were ever going to wake up. How do you feel?" he asked. His voice was kind and Nikki wasn't fearful.

"I… I guess I'm okay." Her throat felt raw, making her tone hoarse, and she tried clearing it, but it did little good.

"I was worried about you. You've been sleeping for almost three days."

"Where am I?"

"Oh, you're at my place. I found you unconscious out there in the snow. You were bleeding from your shoulder and your head."

"Bleeding?"

"Yes, I bandaged you up when I got you here. I think you may have hit your head on a rock, but your shoulder looked like someone shot you. Your jacket has a hole in it and, like I said, your shoulder was bleeding pretty badly."

Nikki touched her shoulder slowly and she felt the bandages. When she touched her temple she found another bandage. She frowned at the man, still wondering where she was.

She told him, "I guess I need to thank you. You must have saved my life."

"In a way, yes. I'm secluded up here, and if I hadn't been out hiking, you could have frozen to death. By the way, my name is Painter, John Painter. What's your name?"

"Hello, Mr. Painter, my name is…." Nikki frowned again, searching her memory. "I… I can't seem to remember my name." She closed her eyes as if she could search her mind to locate her name. She finally realized she couldn't remember anything about herself.

"Oh, god, I can't remember anything!"

"Now, now, don't panic. Your memory will return. I've read that sometimes if a person experiences trauma, they might also experience a loss of memory." Painter's tone was fatherly. "You just relax. You must be hungry since you haven't eaten anything in three days. I've made soup. I'll bring you a bowl.

Nikki laid back, waiting for the soup, and she racked her mind trying to remember something, anything. *Who am I? Where did I come from? Why am I up here someplace where there's snow? Is it winter?* All these questions and more filled her mind.

She felt like crying but she knew it wouldn't do any good and, for some reason, her heart hurt. There was a deep pain, not so much physical as emotional, as if she'd lost someone in death. Maybe someone she loved deeply had died. She placed her hand over her heart and rubbed that part of her chest.

John Painter watched Nikki drink the soup and wondered what a lovely young woman of color was doing in the mountains of Colorado. It had been fortunate that he happened to be hiking in that part of the mountains. He usually walked in another direction, but he'd decided to get a different perspective of the landscape. He'd been working on a painting but for some reason he wasn't feeling inspired.

After Nikki finished her bowl of soup, John took it back and then he quickly returned to the chair so they could talk.

"Since you can't remember your name. Do you think if I start saying different names, you may remember?"

Nikki was sitting up. She propped herself up with her coverings wrapped around her torso. "Yes, that sounds good," she said.

"Okay, here goes. Alice, Alexandra, Betty, Evelyn, Elizabeth, Linda, Sherry, Doris, Ruth, Shannon, Joyce, Carol, or Carolyn." With each name, Nikki just said, "No." Then he said, "Hanna."

Nikki looked at him, "Yes, yes."

"Is that your name?"

"No, but it feels… It makes me feel good here." She placed her hand on her chest. "It's a name that somehow makes me feel safe. Yes, call me Hanna. It's a good name."

From then on, she was Hanna to John Painter. He shared with her that he came to this cabin for a few weeks every winter to work on his wood carvings and painting. "Yes, I know my last name is Painter…and I do paint. But not fences." He then chuckled at his own joke.

He was Native American and lived most of the time in Taos, New Mexico. He was a widower with two grown children and five grandchildren. His wife had died four years ago. This place had been their getaway. Now, he came here to meditate, paint and carve wooden figures.

"Where did you put my clothes?" Nikki asked.

"I patched your jacket with duct tape and sewed your sweater the best I could. Basically, I washed your clothes and what you're wearing is clothing my daughter has left up here. Please don't feel embarrassed. I had to be sure you were all right with no broken ribs. I did nothing inappropriate. I took care of a sick wife for a year before she passed away. I'm an honorable man."

"Thanks, I believe you. So, do you have a phone? Can you call anyone?"

"Nope, no cell service, no landline. We're here until the first week of May. We're about fifteen miles from the nearest town which is Coopersville. I hike, but I'm not up for walking fifteen miles of rugged terrain. We'll be alright."

"Aren't you afraid to be up here alone so far away from everything?"

"No, I like it. If anything were to happen to me, I'd be fine with it." With that statement, he stood. "I'm going to clean up the kitchen and then go to my studio. There are some magazines and books over there on the shelves. Try to make yourself comfortable. There's a small bathroom just past the kitchen. My studio and bedroom are upstairs. There's a little bedroom just on the other side of the fireplace. You're more than welcome to sleep in there or continue on the couch." He then walked back toward what Nikki assumed was the kitchen.

Nikki didn't have the desire or the energy to move. Perplexed about her situation, of having no memory of her name or past, she wondered what she should or could do? Mr. Painter seemed nice but was that all an act? He claimed he didn't touch her in any bad way but could she know that for sure? Then she recalled a dream, and it scared her. It seemed as if she had dreamed it several times. She just couldn't quite put her finger on exactly what was happening in this dream. It frightened her and made her chest hurt.

After John went upstairs, Nikki tried walking around. It would help her become more familiar with her new surroundings. Much of the decor was western and American Indian. The kitchen and dining area were nice with a dining table of fine-grain wood. The four chairs had legs that looked like tree limbs and they had woven seats. The center of the table featured a carved horse that looked as if it were prancing. There were no cabinet doors on the kitchen cabinets. All the spices, dishes, and pots and pans were visible. The cooking utensils were in wide-mouth clay jars and the carving knives were housed in a wooden knife holder. The eating utensils were also in smaller clay jugs. Nikki liked the way everything was organized. She was curious so she opened the refrigerator to see its contents. There were a couple of different cheeses, juice, milk, and various condiments and the pot that the soup was in took up a lot of space. There were also other items, leftovers from previous meals. She noticed that he had another freezer which she discovered was full. Yes, he was apparently ready to stay a long time.

Nikki saw a yellow down jacket with duct tape on the shoulder and surmised it belonged to her. She instinctively rubbed her shoulder which still hurt. She looked out a window to see snow for what seemed to be miles and miles. With a sigh, she went to inspect the bedroom that she would use and the bathroom. Everything was neat, clean, and orderly.

Once she'd finished looking at everything on the ground floor, Nikki returned to the couch which divided the living room from the kitchen. She had found a novel that looked interesting. If this was to be her life for at least now, she may as well make the best of it.

Two days had passed and Nikki's skin was dry. Her hair was lacking moisturizer and she hated the way her fingernails were looking. *This isn't me,* she thought. *I don't know who I am, but I know I take better care of myself than this.*

"Painter," she called out as she ascended the stairs to the second level. When she entered his studio, the bright Colorado sun seemed to stream in even though the windows faced north.

"Yes, Hanna." His focus never left the snowy landscape painting he was working on.

"Do you have any women's lotions, shampoos, or something? I really need lotion after I take a shower. Doesn't your daughter leave any toiletries here?"

"Let me think," he said as he slowly dabbed a little more paint onto the canvas. "I'll check my bathroom." He then purposely placed the paintbrush down before turning to face Nikki. He said in a kidding tone. "Yes, your hair does need help, doesn't it."

Nikki stuck her tongue out at him, which made him chuckle. "Follow me, let's see what we can find."

Nikki walked behind him like an obedient child. Since she'd been here it hadn't taken long for the two of them to feel comfortable in each other's company. Nikki hadn't dared go into Painter's bedroom and now she saw how nice it was. She could see his wife's influence here. It wasn't as masculine as the rest of the house.

"Your wife had good taste," Nikki said as she looked at the beautiful lavender, white, and dark purple quilt, the king-size bed with the fine wood grain headboard, and the large, matching pillow shams. There were two large dressers and in one corner of the room was a window seat with pillows.

"Yes," Painter agreed.

The bathroom had double sinks with drawers under the sinks and cabinets on one wall. A shower big enough for four was on another wall. No bathtub.

"Tell you what, you look through these drawers and in that cabinet. My daughter uses this side of the bathroom when she's here. And there may be some of her stuff. Hopefully, you can find something." Then he smiled. "I have a question. Do women of color have curly wavy hair like yours? I am not trying to be mean, I'm just an ignorant Indian." He leaned back against the door frame folding his muscular arms across his chest.

"Well, Painter, it really depends on the ancestry. If I could remember what mine was, I could tell you more. But I can't, sorry." Nikki shrugged her shoulders. "But I think with racial mixing the hair just reflects the dominant gene. It's all in the genetics."

"Okay, well you look around and I'll be back in my workplace," he said as he turned and walked away.

Nikki began her scavenger hunt. She found a shampoo, a deep conditioner, and a wide tooth comb. Way in the back of the cabinets under the sink was a body lotion but it was very old. She tossed it. She located a small jar of petroleum jelly that wasn't completely empty. She clutched these items to her chest as if she'd found gold. She knew that there was coconut oil in the kitchen, and she could use that, as well. Then she found a fingernail file. *This will work*, Nikki thought as she walked into her bathroom.

She spent the rest of the day on her hair and skincare. Nikki melted the coconut oil just until it became liquid. Then, leaning over the sink in her bathroom, she applied it to her hair and scalp. Then she took plastic wrap and wrapped her hair up. On top of that, she put a towel around her head. After about twenty minutes, she showered while washing her hair. The oil had made her hair soft. She applied the conditioner and then braided her hair. Next, she used coconut oil, mixed with a small amount of petroleum jelly, and rubbed it over her body. She used as little as possible. She didn't know how long she would be in this place.

As the days turned into weeks, Nikki and Painter began to find comfort in each other's company. They would go on hikes together. For Nikki, this seemed a normal activity. She even mentioned to Painter that she felt that she had always been physically active.

"That's interesting because my wife only liked to quilt. I think she would walk with me because she knew I liked it. And I really believe our walks extended her life." Painter said.

"May I ask, how did you meet your wife?" Nikki asked. They were returning from one of their daily hikes.

"Taos isn't that large of a town and she'd just moved there. I was eating at one of the cafes when she walked in with a couple of her friends. I don't know how to explain it but there was something special about her smile. I knew one of the women she was with so I made up my mind to get information," he said, and he paused with a smile. He was recalling that conversation.

"Go on," Nikki urged.

Painter was lost in thought and didn't answer immediately. They continued walking and Nikki waited for him to finish his story. Finally, he shared how the following morning he went to his friend's store as soon as it opened. He asked him the questions that had kept him awake all that previous night. *How old is she? What's her name? Is she single? Is she just visiting or a permanent resident?*

"Goodness, you didn't waste any time getting the information," Nikki said.

"You're so right. And I was glad to learn that she was single, a widow. Her late husband had been killed in an automobile accident about three years before. She was twenty-six years old and had decided to move to Taos for a change of scenery and to forget the bad memories."

"What happened next?"

"I didn't want to rush but I needed to meet her, so I asked my friend to maybe have a get-together. That way she could meet a few people, and I'd have the chance to introduce myself. It took a few days but it happened. My friend, Gayle, had a small dinner party at her house. There were maybe ten to twelve people there. There were also a couple of other single guys there but I made sure that I introduced myself first. Then I stood close to her but not so close that she'd feel uncomfortable. We talked for a long while and I gave her my phone number. I explained that I was busy with my art gallery but that I'd been told that she quilted. I offered to display some of her work in my gallery if she wanted."

"You were smooth," Nikki said.

"Not smooth but hopeful. The other single guys that were there were better looking and one was a doctor. About a week later she phoned and, as they say, the rest is history." Painter grinned.

"That's a nice story. And you two were married for how many years?"

"Almost thirty. It was a good marriage. I don't think I could ever be happier. But she said when she knew she was dying that, if I remarried, she would be okay with it."

They finished their walk in silence. Painter, deep in thought, and Nikki, wondering if she had a love like that in her life.

In April, Painter asked Nikki if she'd pose for him. "There are black people who are mixed with native people. I think I'd like to put you into a native outfit with some feathers in your hair."

"Really! Do you think anyone would believe that I was Indian?"

"I don't care what people think. They'll either like it or not. I just think it would be interesting. So how about it?"

Throughout the month of April and the beginning of May she modeled. She seemed to be a natural at it. She pulled her hair flat, close to her skull, tying it tightly at the nape of her neck. Painter placed beautiful eagle feathers at the back of her head. The buckskin, white-beaded top looked fetching next to Nikki's brown skin. She truly enjoyed working with him, and he was meticulous as he sketched, then began to apply paint. He wouldn't let her see his work during the process.

Unfortunately, every night Nikki continued to have nightmares and each morning she would awaken screaming. It wasn't a loud scream but it caused pain in her chest, close to her heart. The pain wasn't physical, it was emotional pain. She somehow knew that she loved someone with intensity. But who?

Nikki didn't see herself as beautiful because she didn't know who she was. Painter said, "If you don't know who you are, how can you appreciate your beauty? True beauty is internal."

"Painter, is it finished?" Nikki asked.

"Yes, I think I captured your true beauty." Painter said.

Nikki was so surprised as she gazed at the painting. Painter was truly talented. He'd made her brown skin glow with soft red undertones. The position of her head with her eyes looking upward showed a hopeful expression.

"Is that how I look?"

"To me, yes." Painter said unable to hide the pride in his voice.

A few days later, he announced that it was time for them to return to civilization. He began to pack his tools, paints, and canvases. He asked Nikki to box up the canned goods. His son-in-law would be there in a couple of days. He asked her to stack the plates in paper shopping bags except for the two they'd need. Nikki got busy cleaning up the kitchen and storing items that they wouldn't be using. She wiped down all of the shelves in the kitchen and put most of the pots and pans away in the pantry. Painter explained that any canned goods would return with them. They only had one package of frozen meat that they would use for stew. The eggs had been gone for a week, and they'd been drinking soup for breakfast.

BLIND LOVE 001

Nikki thought she would never want another can of soup in her life. She was beginning to feel a sense of joy that she would finally be able to figure out who she was. That dream she had nightly made her think that someone close, someone she loved, had been killed. Maybe she was the only witness to a killing. She was becoming anxious with the idea of finding out what and who she really was.

CHAPTER 9

Good News/ Bad News

The sheriff's office was busier than usual. State troopers were talking in low voices when Jami and Hannibal along with Max entered the main area. Troopers nodded in their direction and some even said a greeting. Jami's nerves were on edge because there hadn't been any news. Each day Jami phoned, and the Sheriff's assistant apologized but said, "I'm so sorry, Mr. Bledsoe, but we've heard nothing. I promise you, as soon as Sheriff Bronson hears anything, we'll let you know."

Now the call. Sheriff Bronson was standing in the doorway of his office and he motioned for them to come in. Max leads Jami into the office with Hannibal following. A deputy and a detective were standing close to the sheriff's desk.

"Jami, you may want to sit down. We've got good news and bad news. Which would you want to hear first?"

Jami cleared his throat as he felt it suddenly tighten. He sat in the chair in front of the sheriff's desk. "Give me the good news first."

"Okay, we located that stolen rental vehicle early this morning. There was an avalanche some time ago on one of the back roads. The snowplow was clearing the road and found the jeep. There were only two bodies, both male and have been identified as the escaped convicts we've been searching for."

"And the bad news?"

"We haven't found Nikki. We've still got people searching but to be honest, I'm not hopeful."

Jami couldn't speak. What does this mean? Did they kill her and dump her body someplace? He couldn't move. It was as if his legs wouldn't hold his weight. Placing both of his hands over his face Jami leaned forward and inhaled deeply. She's not dead, he told himself. She can't be.

He sat upright and exhaled as he looked at the sheriff. Finally, he said, "Thanks, Sheriff, I appreciate all that you and your men have been doing for me and our families. A question—is there any possibility that she may have survived? Nikki is a strong woman."

"Jami, there's always a chance but where we found the vehicle there are no cabins or shelters nearby. Maybe you should return to Chicago and be with your family and friends. You need to heal."

"I appreciate what you're saying and perhaps we will. But I'm still holding on to the hope that she's alive and that I will have her back in my arms." Jami then stood up, thanking everyone again.

Hannibal had said nothing the entire time they were inside the sheriff's office. The news of finding the vehicle stabbed his heart. His hope had been fading during the weeks of waiting. Now, with this information, he was ready to leave Colorado and never return. For him, it had become a place of sorrow.

"Now what, Jami?" he asked.

"One more week, Hannibal. Then we'll go back to Chicago. She'll be with us. I can feel it in my bones. Contact a cleaning service and have them get our house ready."

"Jami, are you insane? Did you hear what the sheriff said? There were only two bodies. Where would she be if she wasn't with those cons?"

"She escaped. I know I sound insane, but I just know it."

Jami decided not to phone the families—yet. He had to wait because he needed to share good news. After all, it was just the first week of May.

BENNA ELSE

For Nikki, the first week of May was her ticket to learning more about herself. Painter explained that his son-in-law would arrive in the evening. They would load most of the boxes in the bed of the pick-up. Then they'd spend the night and get up early to leave the next morning.

The look on Ryan's face when he saw Nikki was priceless. Both Painter and Nikki laughed hard. Then Painter explained all that had happened and how Nikki came to be staying with him.

"So, you can't remember anything?" Ryan asked.

"Not really," Nikki said. "Lately, I've been having some thoughts but nothing is clear. I'm hoping once we get to town I can talk to the police or sheriff. Maybe they can help me."

"I can't wait to tell this story to my wife," Ryan said.

Painter smiled. "I'll just bet you can't."

After their last meal of stew, Nikki washed the dishes and the men began loading boxes into the truck. The cabin looked so strange with everything put away. Nikki showered, using the last of her homemade cosmetics. Finally, getting into bed she seemed to recall someone saying, "...*our love is blind...,*" And she felt a flutter in the area of her chest near her heart.

Slowly she drifted off to sleep. But tonight her dream was different. There was a dog, a friendly dog, and there was laughter. In the morning, she awoke with her quiet scream and a name that she had said in the dream. Awake she just couldn't recall that name.

Painter, Ryan, and Nikki piled into the cab of the truck. The roads were mostly clear. There was still snow on the high mountain ranges but in most of the valleys, green grass was visible. Nikki liked what she saw. "This is beautiful," she said.

"Maybe, once you get your memory back, you'll come up here. There's a ski resort not far from Coopersville."

"I think I'd like that," Nikki told him.

"Hanna, before we go to the sheriff's office, we need to eat something. I know this wonderful breakfast place and we'll go there before I turn you over to the authorities," Painter teased.

"That's fine with me."

BLIND LOVE 001

⁓⁕⁓

The week was up and Hannibal had packed everything. The car was gassed up and he was ready to hit the road. Jami was sullen. He'd always depended on his instincts, especially when it came to his wife. Now he was leaving without her. He still had not phoned anyone but he'd received calls. It was on the news that two bodies had been found after weeks of searching by the different law enforcement agencies. Dave called first, then her parents, and finally his dad. Jami couldn't really talk. What could he say? He'd agreed to return home but he didn't like it.

"Hannibal, let's eat breakfast before we get on the road. I've enjoyed the restaurant that has those wonderful pancakes. Nikki and I ate there a few times."

Nikki, Painter, and Ryan finished their meals and were leaving the restaurant. Painter was right, the food was outstanding. They were happy that they'd gotten there early because there was a small crowd waiting to be seated.

⁓⁕⁓

Hannibal and Jami were waiting for a table. As a few people were leaving, Hannibal told Jami that it shouldn't be long. Then Hannibal excused himself to go to the men's room. Jami and Max were waiting when Max whimpered. It wasn't the same whimper he'd make for Jami, it was Nikki's whimper.

⁓⁕⁓

As Painter, Ryan, and Nikki squeezed past the waiting crowd she noticed a good-looking, brown-skinned man with a dog. He looked familiar but she kept walking toward the restaurant exit.

⁓⁕⁓

"Max! Where's Nikki?" Jami said urgently. He recognized Max's whimper for Nikki. He wondered if Max had found Nikki just as he'd found him below the cliff.

Suddenly, Max nearly jerked Jami down, as he bolted outside. Jami ran and began yelling Nikki's name while Max continued pulling him along.

Nikki heard a man's voice calling a name. She turned around.

Screaming, "Jami, Jami!" She ran to him. Her memory had returned in that instant. She ran into his outstretched arms.

He hugged her, they kissed, and they both cried. Max was so excited, he kept barking and jumping up and down.

Hannibal came out of the men's room just in time to see Jami being pulled by Max. He ran after them. *What is going on?*

Then he saw Nikki and stopped in disbelief. She was alive!

Painter and Ryan watched as Hanna had separated from them and had run into the arms of a tall, good-looking man. They noticed the dog had a harness identifying him as a service dog, and they watched in amazement as another man joined them. All of them were hugging and crying.

"You're alive, you're alive!" That's all Jami could seem to say for the moment. His emotions were over the top. His wife was back in his arms.

"Nikki, how did this happen?" Hannibal asked after hugging Nikki, his eyes tearing up.

"Oh, goodness, I was rescued." Then she turned around without leaving Jami's embrace.

"Painter, Ryan, come meet my husband and his friend."

The two men ambled toward the threesome. It was obvious that Painter knew that Hanna's memory had returned and he seemed very happy for her. Ryan seemed to not have a clue of what was going on.

"Jami, this is Painter. He saved my life," Nikki said, and then she introduced everyone else, even Max.

Jami shook hands with Painter. "What can I say but thank you for saving my wife!"

Painter smiled, then looked at the woman he had known as Hanna. "So, your name is Nikki?"

"Yes, my name is Nikki Bledsoe, and I'm married to the most wonderful man. We haven't been married for a full year yet."

Jami felt overwhelmed. "I want to hear the whole story of this rescue. But, I think we all should go to the sheriff's office," he suggested. "I'm very sure he wants to learn of this great development."

⁂

The normally stoic female deputy seemed to not believe her eyes when she saw the group entering the office. Jami was beaming and holding onto his wife. He asked if the sheriff was in.

"He is and I can't wait to see his face," she said as she picked up the phone to call him.

When Sheriff Bronson came out of his office door, he stopped in shocked disbelief. "Damn, *Nikki!*" he shouted. Moving quickly, he gave her a big hug. "My god, girl, I never thought I'd see you again." Then he looked at the little group around her. "Well, all of you come on in. I know this is a story I gotta hear."

The five of them followed the sheriff into his office. Nikki and Jami sat in the chairs in front of the sheriff's desk. Painter, Ryan, and Hannibal found a place on the worn leather couch that was along the wall across from the desk. Jami continued holding Nikki's hand while Max lay down by their feet.

"Well, tell me, how did this come about?" the sheriff asked. "And John Painter, how are you involved in this?"

"I guess I'd better start," Nikki said. "After knocking Jami unconscious, they made me fix food. I refused and they threatened to kill my husband. He'd already fired a shot so close to Jami's head that I was sure he would do what he said. So, I fixed the meal and after they ate, they forced me into the car. I was scared. They put me in the passenger seat, then the taller one drove while the other guy sat in the backseat. He was holding the gun.

All I could think of was Jami. I needed to get back to the cabin. He was hurt and so I tried to figure out a way to escape.

The roads were slippery and he was driving too fast. He hit an icy patch and lost control of the car. We ended up facing in the opposite direction. The driver-side door pushed into a snowbank. That meant I needed to get out before he could get out. As they fussed with each other and tried to get the car unstuck, I gradually moved away from them. Then I turned and ran. They realized that I was getting away. I didn't want them to have a clear shot at me so I jumped from the roadway and down the side of the slope.

The snow was so deep that it was above my knees. I could barely lift my feet but I wasn't going to let them get me. Then I heard the first gunshot. I didn't look back even though they were yelling at me. I thought, if they wanted me bad enough they were going to have to come after me.

The second shot got me and I fell down. I think I must have rolled. The slope was pretty steep. I just felt a sharp pain in my shoulder but somehow, I forced myself to keep moving.

Then I remember tripping and that's all I recall until I woke up at Painter's cabin."

"Oh, Babe," Jami said softly, as he gently squeezed her hand.

The sheriff asked Painter, "So how did you happen to find her?"

Painter cleared his throat before speaking. "I usually hike a little daily but for some reason, I hiked farther than usual. When I was just about ready to turn around and head back home, I saw a clump of bright yellow in the white snow. Curious, I headed towards it, and there she was. There was dried blood on her forehead, and I could see more on the torn shoulder of her jacket. She had frostbite on her cheeks. At first, I thought she was dead. When I realized she wasn't, I carried her back to my place. I'm not a young man and it took a while but we made it back.

I had removed her jacket and I saw that she had a shoulder wound. It looked as if her shoulder had a graze. So I removed her sweater, cleaned up that wound on her shoulder, and then I cleaned and patched up her head wound.

It was a good thing she was wearing good-quality gear because she could have frozen to death. Anyway, I placed her on my couch and wrapped her in a blanket and quilt. I moved the couch a little closer to the fireplace, and she slept for three days. Finally, she woke up."

"You mean to tell me that she slept that long?" Sheriff Bronson asked.

"Yep, and then once she felt like talking, she couldn't remember her name or where she came from. It was weird."

Between Nikki and Painter, they explained how they co-existed for the rest of their time together. Painter also brought up how he only knew Nikki by the name of Hanna.

"Yes, when Painter said that he had to give me a name, since I couldn't remember my own, he started calling out various names. When he said Hanna, I said stop. There was something about the sound of that name that gave me a secure feeling." Nikki looked in Hannibal's direction. "I think because it was close to Hannibal, and he is our security."

Everyone turned to look at an embarrassed Hannibal, but he also felt a sense of pride.

"What I don't understand is why didn't you contact anyone?" Jami asked.

"I don't have a phone or any means of contacting anyone when I'm up in my cabin. You see, Mr. Bledsoe, that place is my retreat. I really don't have contact with the outside world for about three to four months. I'm a painter and I can concentrate better that way. Also, it was a place that was special to me and my late wife. So, you see, until my son-in-law comes for me, I'm just there."

"I can verify that, Jami," the sheriff said. "John Painter comes every winter to stay. He usually has enough provisions to last him for five months. Unfortunately, his cabin didn't come into our search area and to be honest, I really didn't think about him."

There was a lull in the conversation, then the sheriff stood up and smiled. "I always like a happy ending to a story. And believe me, this story will be in the papers very soon. Jami, I guess you were right. And I'm so glad you were." He walked from behind his desk where he'd been sitting and hugged Nikki and then Jami. He shook hands with the others and gave Max a loving pat on his head.

⁂

As they left the building, Jami expressed his deep appreciation to John Painter. He also invited him to come visit them in Chicago. Painter laughed, saying he wasn't a city boy, but he thanked Jami for the invite. Before they parted, Nikki got her yellow jacket from the truck. It had been too warm to wear on this early spring day.

After leaving the sheriff's office in their car, both Jami and Hannibal realized that they hadn't eaten anything. Hannibal decided that they needed to get on the road. "Once we get close to Denver, we'll stop and eat. You two need to be making phone calls. I'm sure your families want to hear everything."

Jami had phoned the house rental agent that morning. to let her know they were leaving. Now called her to let her know that his wife had been found and that they needed to return to the house for a couple of hours.

When they entered the house, Nikki was pleasantly surprised that Hannibal had her suitcase with Jami's. She opened it to find her own clothes. She put on familiar, comfortable apparel, and smiled, content with having found *herself* and *her life* again.

"Nikki," Hannibal said after he'd knocked on the bedroom door.

"Hannibal, come in, I'm just so happy. How can I ever thank you? You saved Jami, your name was in my head. You are one of the best people I know."

"Well, thanks, but I have something I need to give you." Hannibal's voice was emotional.

Just then Jami came into the room and sensed that something was about to happen. He'd just finished speaking to the agent.

"Is everything okay?" Jami asked.

"Yeah, it's just that I've had these since the first day I arrived here," Hannibal said as he reached into his jacket pocket. He held his hand out toward Nikki.

"My rings!" Nikki said as tears came to her eyes

"I found them at the cabin when I was trying to find you both," Hannibal said with his shy smile. "I'd hoped that I would be giving them back to you. But unlike your husband, my hope wasn't as strong, so I'd planned on giving them to Jami when we returned to Chicago. I'm glad to be giving the rings back to their rightful owner now."

Nikki, gently taking the rings out of Hannibal's hand, hugged him tightly. "Thank you, my dear, dear friend."

"Wow, Hannibal, you are an even better man than I thought. Thank you, man." Jami said.

During the drive to Denver, Jami and Nikki were busy calling family and friends. Screams and tears of joy filled the car. The long-awaited meal was perfect. Then they checked into a motel outside of Denver. Nikki showered using her special toiletries with the fragrances Jami loved. In bed, Nikki said, "You know, you never told me how you were found. What happened?"

Jami explained his story and Nikki cried. He held her tight because she blamed herself for all that had happened.

"It's alright, Babe. I'm fine, you're fine. We're both alive. And I learned to ski. And wasn't that our goal?" he teased. Then he kissed her tear-covered cheeks and then her mouth. They made love.

POSTSCRIPT

That summer, after Hannibal returned from cooking school in Paris, Jami and Nikki went to visit John Painter in Taos. The painting of Nikki as a native hung in a prominent spot in his gallery.

"Wow, that's beautiful," Hannibal exclaimed.

Nikki explained to Jami the details of the painting. Jami could make out some of it but, from Hannibal's reaction alone, Jami offered to buy it.

"No, Jami," Painter said. "I can't part with it. Your wife helped me at a time I was going through a deep depression. If I hadn't found her, I would not be here. I tell you what—when I die, I'll will it to you."

The following winter, they returned to ski. This time, Hannibal insisted on being with them for the whole trip.

Two years later, Nikki and Jami became parents to fraternal twins, a boy named Jonathan Jamison "J.J." Bledsoe, and a girl named Hanna Nicole Bledsoe.

THE END